THE BRIDE, THE BABY AND THE BEST MAN

In three weeks' time, Faith Bridges will marry safe, dependable, practical Julian. Their plans don't include children — just a nice, calm, platonic marriage. But then along comes Harry March, one adorable baby, and one cute four-year-old. Harry is definitely not safe — he's sexy, rude, impractical and utterly charming. He might have been best man material, but he isn't Faith's type at all . . . And as soon as she can stop herself kissing Harry she will tell him so!

LIZ FIELDING

THE BRIDE, THE BABY AND THE BEST MAN

Complete and Unabridged

LINFORD
Leicester

First published in Great Britain in 1996

First Linford Edition
published 2012

All the characters in this book have no existence
outside the imagination of the author, and have
no relation whatsoever to anyone bearing the
same name or names. They are not even distantly
inspired by any individual known or unknown to
the author, and all the incidents are purely
invention.

British Library CIP Data

Fielding, Liz.
 The bride, the baby and the best man. - -
(Linford romance library)
 1. Love stories.
 2. Large type books.
 I. Title II. Series
 823.9′14–dc23

 ISBN 978–1–4448–1359–3

Published by
F. A. Thorpe (Publishing)
Anstey, Leicestershire

Set by Words & Graphics Ltd.
Anstey, Leicestershire
Printed and bound in Great Britain by
T. J. International Ltd., Padstow, Cornwall

This book is printed on acid-free paper

1

'Blackmail,' Faith muttered for perhaps the tenth time that day. Her aunt was an expert in the technique. One of these days she'd call her bluff . . . except, of course, that she wasn't bluffing. She never bluffed. But, whatever crisis had befallen Harry March, Faith vowed that it wouldn't occupy one minute more than twenty-four hours of her precious time. 'Not one second longer,' she remarked to the signpost she had slowed to consult, just to emphasise the point.

But, despite the urgency of the call for help, there was no enthusiastic rush to greet her when she drew up before the small stone manor house that seemed almost to hang from its wooded hillside perch above the river, dominating the well-kept estate that stretched for acres in all directions — timeless, peaceful and quite beautiful. Faith reminded herself that she was long past the age when she could be impressed by such evidence of wealth, or the man who possessed it, and tugged at an old-fashioned wrought-iron bell pull.

For a moment nothing happened, then she heard a faint far-off jangle in some distant servants' hall. All impressively picturesque and charming, no doubt, she thought — like the house, like the stunning bird's-eye view over the woods to the river glinting silver in the evening light below her. Not terribly efficient, of course, but precisely what she would have expected from a man whose reaction to an emergency was to send for his old nanny.

The door was finally opened by a man of military bearing. 'Yes, miss?' The accent was unexpectedly Scottish, the tone dour, the expression lugubrious rather than welcoming.

She opened her mouth to explain her business but was interrupted. 'Mac? Is it her? Don't keep her waiting on the doorstep, man; bring her in.' The crisp tones of a disembodied voice raised impatiently above the more insistent cry of a baby that grew louder as it came nearer cut off her attempt to introduce herself. A baby?

The man who had opened the door regarded her doubtfully for a moment, then turned away. 'It's not Miss Bridges, sir; it's a *young* female.' 'Young' was clearly not a recommendation.

'I'm Faith — '

'Young?' The owner of the voice obviously shared this opinion. But as Harry March appeared in the open doorway of a room leading from the hall, the comfortable shabbiness of which could only have accumulated through generations of hard use, Faith's attempt to explain her presence died on her lips.

The man she had come to help was, according to her aunt, irresistible. But Faith had never doubted her ability to resist the smooth, boyish good looks and too obvious charm that oozed from

3

the photograph in the silver frame that had pride of place on her aunt's sofa-table.

Foolishly, she had expected him to look just the same as a ten-year-old photograph. Ten years was not long and men, after all, changed less than women in the decade between their early twenties and thirties. But time had dealt harshly with Harry March, although he still made a singularly striking figure by anybody's calculation.

He was tall — far taller than she had imagined from his picture. It must be because he was so beautifully proportioned, she decided, and had the broad, balancing shoulders of an athlete and a strongly muscled neck to support the kind of head that more usually adorned the warrior statues of ancient Greece. But pain had forged the smoothly handsome features, whittling away at the carefree good looks until all that remained was tough, weather-beaten skin stretched tight across bone — fierce, uncompromising bone that revealed a strength of character she would never have imagined from the softer features in that smiling portrait taken in his youth.

The confident curve of his smile had hardened to a straight line, the slight droop of the lower lip retaining only a suspicion of the reckless sensuality that had dared girls to resist his charm. His nose, long and once arrow-straight, showed a certain battle fatigue and his chin, deeply cleft, boasted such stubbornness that she almost flinched. But dominating the whole was a scar, livid against the tanned outdoor complexion — a scar that scythed from the centre of his forehead to his temple. No longer a pretty face, she thought, remembering her own instinctive recoil from such blatant and careless charm, but one that had been lived in and lived in hard. And the effect on Faith was far more devastating than the unmarked beauty that it had replaced.

She had no time to analyse the odd little skip of her heartbeat, however, no time to shield herself from the heat that flickered unexpectedly through her veins as his vivid cornflower-blue eyes swept over her. She was jerked from her contemplation of the appearance of Harry March by the red-faced infant lying in the crook of his arm, who, having screwed himself up to some special pitch of anguish, let out a cry of such passionate intensity that he gained the undivided attention of all present.

Faith, a career woman to her fingertips who had for reasons of her own made a point of avoiding babies, ignored the little tug of longing deep within her and, clinging to her shoulder bag, kept her distance. Nevertheless she felt compelled to say something. 'What on earth is the matter with the poor thing?' she demanded. No answer being forthcoming, she rushed on. 'Where did it come from?'

'Don't you know?' Harry's mouth twisted briefly in a provoking smile.

'Of course I — ' Too late Faith realised the trap and found herself colouring. 'I meant . . . well, it's not yours, is it?'

'He.'

'What?'

'*He*,' Harry repeated. 'Not *it*.'

'Oh, right. It's just — I didn't think you were married . . . ' Not just didn't think. Knew. Knew he'd jilted the beautiful Clementine Norwood days before their marriage. Called the whole thing off. Her aunt had been going to the wedding. She had bought a special outfit that had cost her a fortune but she'd justified the expense by the fact that she would wear it for Faith's wedding too. It had been a bad year for weddings all round that year . . .

'Who the devil *are* you?' he demanded, his eyes sweeping her with a fierce, raking glance. Then some kind of understanding crossed his face. 'Oh, good grief, you're another of my sister's doe-eyed blondes,' he declared bitterly. 'That's all I need right now.'

'One of your sister's . . . ?' For a moment words failed her. But only for a moment. 'Tell me, Mr March, does she keep a supply in a cupboard for use in emergencies?' Stupid question. This *was* an emergency, wasn't it? At least, her aunt had said it was.

'Not content with lumbering me with her offspring,' Harry March continued, ignoring her question, 'she's back on a matchmaking jag. Well, you've picked the wrong day to call, lady,' he said, walking around her, a slight limp betraying that his injuries extended beyond the scar etched across his forehead. 'As you can see, I'm otherwise engaged.' The baby, as if to emphasise his point, let out another howl of anguish.

'From the look of you, any woman would come in handy right now,' Faith replied coolly. 'Blonde or otherwise.'

'I'm not that desperate, madam. Help is at hand.' He continued to glare at her, jogging the baby more in hope than expectation of its doing any good. Faith found herself taking half a step forward, wanting to do something but unsure what would help. 'Well?' he continued impatiently. 'Let's get it over with. What excuse have you managed to drum up to cover your arrival on my doorstep? You've lost your way, perhaps? That's a favourite.' He didn't bother to disguise his scorn. 'Or do you have some desperate need to use the telephone?'

'It can't be that, sir,' Mac intervened, apparently deriving some dour amusement from the situation. 'The last young lady who dropped by used that as an excuse.'

Harry glanced at Mac. 'Did she? Was that the one with the teeth like gravestones?'

'A slight exaggeration.'

Harry turned back to Faith. 'Come on, out with it. I'm considering a prize for the most original reason for knocking on my door over a six-month period. Today's young women have so little imagination that if you can come up with something amusing it should be yours for the taking.'

Faith, who had been listening to the man with growing irritation, finally snapped. 'Frankly I can't think of a thing you might have that I could possibly want. You said help was at hand, Mr March. Well, what you see is what you get. Take it or leave it. And for your information,' she added, with what she considered remarkable restraint considering the provocation, 'I am *not* a doe-eyed blonde.'

The slightest lift of his eyebrows, however, did nothing for her blood pressure. 'I'll be the judge of that,' he said. 'I was once acknowledged to be an expert on the subject.'

'That's not much of a character reference.'

'Possibly not,' he agreed, unmoved, 'but then I never claimed to be perfect.'

'Very wise of you.'

'I never claimed to be that either, but when I called Janet for help it was because I wanted *her*, not some flibbertigibbet female. And you are not Janet Bridges,' he said accusingly.

'Ten out of ten for observation,' she replied, somewhat drily. Whatever blunt instrument had been used in an attempt to scalp him had clearly not affected his eyesight, even if he was incapable of distinguishing between blonde and the somewhat common-place shade of streaky mouse that represented her crowning glory. 'But I am her niece and if I were a flibbertigibbet she certainly wouldn't have sent me in her place. In fact, Mr March, you'll be relieved to hear that I am positively renowned for my level-headedness.'

'A level-headed woman?' He made no effort to disguise his disbelief. 'Now that *is* original. Although someone being *renowned* for level-headedness seems to me a contradiction in terms.'

Faith had a suspicion that he was right, but she wasn't about to admit it. 'You can take my word for it,' she assured him. 'My level-headedness is spoken of with hushed awe.' Although, she had to admit, not in the world of babycare.

'I'll make up my own mind, thank you, although I would have thought I could have trusted Janet . . . ' He stopped. 'Oh, I see. This is a joint effort. Elizabeth and Janet have used my predicament to entrap me.' He raised his eyes appealingly to the ceiling. 'Heaven spare me from the machinations of all women. Especially the ones who think they are acting for your own good.'

Faith, hungry and tired from a long day that had culminated in this dash into rural England instead of the anticipated pleasure of shopping in Knightsbridge with her two best friends, had not been expecting to be welcomed with a pipe band, but neither was she amused by her less than enthusiastic reception. In fact she was positively annoyed, but since she was also an acknowledged expert at keeping her thoughts to herself Harry March had no way of knowing that.

'Heaven has been merciful on this occasion, Mr March, although why it should bother itself with you when you're quite so impossibly rude is beyond me. I have never met your sister, and if she is seeking to inflict you

12

and your bad manners upon some poor unsuspecting female then frankly I don't much want to. Janet certainly has more sense.' Or had she? Aunt Janet had made no secret of her disapproval of Faith's forthcoming marriage. But surely she wouldn't stoop to such underhand tactics . . . ?

The baby, who had momentarily ceased yelling in order to contemplate her with large blue eyes, opened his mouth and began to make his presence felt once more. 'Is he hungry?' she enquired tentatively, partly in an effort to be helpful, partly to take her mind off the uncomfortable feeling that her aunt was perfectly capable of trying to upset her wedding plans. She had once described Harry as irresistible. Maybe she hoped he would be.

'I fed and changed him, miss,' Mac informed her.

Faith turned thankfully to the dour Scot, hardly surprised that that particular task had been delegated by Harry. He was, no doubt, a past master at the

13

art. At something of a loss as to any other likely cause of the infant's distress, she asked, 'And you closed the nappy pins?'

'I used one of those disposable things. They don't have pins.'

'Disposable?' Faith repeated with exasperation. 'Have you any idea of the landfill problems caused by — ' She stopped. This was hardly the moment for a lecture in environmental correctness and the pathetic yells were beginning to tug uncomfortably at some deeply instinctive feelings within her. Despite herself, she took another step closer. 'Can't you stop it crying?' she demanded of Harry.

'I've been attempting to do that most of the day, but since you're here to help you can have a try.' With that he dumped the baby in her arms. 'His name is Ben.'

He was so small, so defenceless, so loud. And she didn't have a clue what to do. 'But . . . ' She held him out to Harry with a helpless little gesture.

Harry ignored it.

'I don't believe I know yours,' he added.

Faith, perfectly at home with a balance sheet or a company report, tried to ignore the yelling and think. More by instinct than any real idea of what to do, she put the infant over her shoulder and began to pat his back. Ben dug his tiny nails into her shoulder and was promptly sick over it. But he stopped crying. She kept very still, afraid that any untoward movement might start him off again, afraid that he might throw up again. Instead he lifted his wobbly head and looked at her before yawning mightily and falling asleep with his warm, damp head tucked trustingly against her neck.

'Oh, well done,' Mac said.

'Well done? But he's been sick all over me,' she whispered fiercely, the dampness beginning to seep through the silk of her shirt.

Harry looked over her shoulder. 'It's not much,' he informed her.

15

She looked up. 'That's easy for you to say . . . ' she began, then, because his eyes were uncomfortably close to hers, she shifted her gaze to the sleeping infant and was immediately enchanted by the delicate curve of long dark lashes on a downy cheek. Once she had longed for a family of her own, then Michael had cut loose and run a week before their wedding. After that, refusing to be hurt ever again, she had blocked her mind to love, romance, a family of her own and concentrated on her career. Yet this little creature seemed to catch at something deep within her, tugging dangerously at her heartstrings.

She looked up, saw the two men looking at her with a knowing expression, and she blushed slightly and stiffened. 'Right, Mr March, if that was what all the fuss was about I'll be on my way.'

'Who are you? Really.' Now that Ben had stopped crying and the immediate crisis was over Harry's features had relaxed slightly into the possibility of a smile. Faith avoided the temptation to respond in kind.

'I'm Faith Bridges. Janet Bridges is my aunt. *Really.*'

'I see. It runs in the family, does it?' He indicated the sleeping child. 'Being able to handle yelling babies?'

'Not in this family. I work for a bank.' Worked. She still hadn't quite got used to her freedom.

Harry's dark brows peaked in surprise. 'By choice?'

'Why not?' she demanded indignantly.

'Extraordinary.'

The fact that his surprise was clearly genuine didn't make it any less insulting. 'What's extraordinary about it? It certainly beats wiping dirty noses and bottoms for a living.' She reached up and eased the wet silk away from her shoulder as if to emphasise her point.

His smile was definitely widening. 'Put like that, I'm prepared to concede you may have a point. But most women

17

can't wait to do it, even without a pay cheque at the end of the month.'

'I am not most women.'

'No?' He regarded the tender way she held the child and dismissed her protestations with a disbelieving look. 'Well, the nursery suite is on the first floor, second door on the left. You'll find everything you'll need in there.' He didn't wait for her response but turned to Mac. 'I don't know about you but I could do with a drink.'

Faith stood for a moment open-mouthed as he turned towards the library. Then she found her voice.

'Excuse me!'

'Yes?' As Harry turned his dark blue eyes upon her she wavered. But only for a moment.

'The only thing I need right now is the door out of here. So if you'll kindly take the baby I'll be on my way.'

'But you've only just arrived!' Harry exclaimed, apparently impatient for his drink. 'I told Janet that I needed her for at least a week.'

'A week!' Of all the conniving, blackmailing manipulative old women . . . She *knew* that was impossible! 'I can't spare a week — '

'Then you should have told her that before you came. In fact you never told me why she didn't come herself.'

Faith felt herself sinking into boggy ground. Janet had made her promise not to tell Harry about her operation, although she wasn't sure that her aunt deserved such loyalty under the circumstances. 'She retired two years ago, Mr March, when it all got a bit much for her,' she said, sidestepping the question. 'And she seems to have forgotten to mention anything about staying for a week. Or babies.'

He looked disbelieving. 'She sounded perfectly rational when I spoke to her. And she was as fit as a fiddle last time I saw her.'

'And when was that?' she snapped back, and was gratified by the tightening of the muscles that clamped his jaw shut. 'Anyway, I thought you had already made up your mind that I was sent by your sister to lure you up the aisle?' she added caustically. 'Since you're clearly not interested, I might as well be on my way.'

His eyes gleamed in the dusky evening light. 'Oh, no, Faith Bridges. You look right, but you're altogether too sharp-tongued for that particular game. But if Janet could have come she would, retired or not. So why did she send you in her place?'

He was so sure of his authority, his power to command instant attention that Faith felt an urgent desire to dent his arrogance. She restrained herself. 'She had other commitments that she couldn't avoid, Mr March, but she asked me to try and sort out your problems as best I could. Since I've absolutely no experience as a nanny my advice is that you do what you should have done in the first place and call an agency.'

'An agency?'

'A nanny agency. There are dozens of

them in the Yellow Pages. Since this is your sister's child, why don't you ask her to help you find one? Where is she, anyway?'

'My sister is in America. I told — '

'She went away and left it with you?' Faith's disbelief was palpable and ignited a dangerous spark in his eye.

'It's only for a few days,' he said, glaring at Mac when he would have interrupted, 'and it was Elizabeth's idea to call Janet.' Then quite suddenly he smiled. It was an assured, I-can-get-away-with-anything smile, just the kind of smile to captivate a recalcitrant female, and Faith suspected it had been used to devastating effect on more than one occasion. It was a slightly crumpled version these days, to be sure, but if you were in the least bit susceptible . . .

Faith discovered her mouth was softening into a response and had to shake herself mentally, remind herself firmly that she was twenty-five years old, with a considerable reputation for being anything but susceptible. On the contrary, she told herself, she was furious that he would think her so gullible. Unaware of the effect it was causing, he turned and walked back towards her. 'Surely Janet meant you to stay? Otherwise why would she have sent you in her place?'

His logic was impeccable but for one minor detail. 'If she'd understood the nature of the problem I imagine she would have made some other arrangements.'

'Understood the problem?' His eyes narrowed. 'She's a nanny, for heaven's sake; what other reason could I possibly have for asking her to help out?'

Not susceptible, huh? As someone frequently applauded for her objectivity why hadn't she been able to see that for herself? Had she been thinking too much about the man rather than the problem? 'I knew this was a mistake,' she muttered, feeling very stupid. 'I wanted to telephone, but she knew I wouldn't come if I discovered the true nature of the problem; that was why she threatened — '

'Threatened?' He was on the word like a terrier on a rat. There was nothing wrong with his hearing either. 'What exactly did she threaten you with?'

She bit her lower lip as she realised she had very nearly given the game away, and, shifting the sleeping child into the crook of her arm, she offered him to Harry. 'Look, I'm really very sorry, Mr March, but even if I knew the first thing about children I just don't have a week to spare. I simply have to get back to London.'

'Ask for a week's leave,' he said, quite reasonable. 'On compassionate grounds. Or are you going to tell me that you are indispensable, that the bank couldn't possibly manage without you for a whole week?'

He wasn't insulting her, she realised, but teasing, and disconcertingly she blushed. 'It's not the bank. I've left my job. It's personal business — '

'Couldn't you handle it from here?' Harry ignored the proffered baby and she took a desperate step closer, which was plainly silly, since she had to tilt her head to look up into his eyes and that made her feel oddly vulnerable — certainly too vulnerable to explain why she had to organise her wedding single-handed. While technically it was perfectly possible to do most things from Wickham Ash, she certainly had no desire to do them under Harry March's taunting eyes.

'The minute I get back to London I'll telephone an agency for you and ask them to despatch a temporary nanny,' she promised.

His smile took on a coaxing quality. He could, apparently, turn it on like a tap. The knowledge didn't make the effect any less devastating. 'That all seems rather unnecessary now you're here. And despite your protestations about your lack of experience you obviously have a way with you. Ben seems to like you; that's worth a lot. I'd pay you top rates,' he said. 'You would have your own sitting room,' he offered temptingly. 'There's a television set there and you can use Elizabeth's car any time you want, and the swimming pool when I'm not using it — '

'I don't need your money,' she said quickly, sensing that she was being steamrollered for the second time that day. 'And I have my own car.' She glanced down at Ben as he sighed in his sleep.

'An Alfa Romeo Spyder, sir,' Mac interjected, with a certain dour satisfaction. 'A red one with a black hood. Very nice.' Harry March ditched the smile and threw him a warning look that would have silenced thunder.

'And I swim every day at my club,' Faith added, as if that settled the matter.

'I don't suppose you have the entire pool to yourself?'

'No, but then I like company. And I never watch television.'

'Never?'

Hardly ever, she amended, but silently, inside her head. 'Who has the time?' she murmured.

'I see.' The words had a slightly

ominous ring as Harry March finally decided to take her objections seriously and give her the benefit of his undivided attention. 'So, I can't tempt you with money or material things? I wonder what would buy you, Faith Bridges?' His eyes were thoughtful, his look assessing. To be inspected quite so thoroughly was disconcerting to say the least, and Faith squirmed under his intense gaze.

'I'm not for sale, Harry March,' she said crossly, longing to turn and walk out of the house, but, still hampered as she was by the baby, escape was impossible.

'Maybe no one has ever offered you something you wanted enough,' he suggested.

'Considering I've driven all the way from London in answer to your cry for help you could at least try to be civil,' she snapped.

'Well, I'm sure it's very good of you to have come all this way just to say you can't help. But something about it worries me a little. You see, I just can't understand why you'd bother.'

'Aunt Janet just said you had some sort of crisis. Unfortunately she didn't say what it was — '

'And are you always so willing to help out in a crisis? It seems excessively altruistic to come all this way to help a perfect stranger.'

Except Harry March wasn't a *stranger*, not in the true sense of the word. Long ago he had been Aunt Janet's favourite nursery charge and she had been telling Faith tales about her darling boy for as long as Faith could remember. And while her aunt might think the sun shone out of his eyes Faith didn't think he was within a country mile of being *perfect*. 'I told you — '

He wasn't interested in what she had told him. 'I'm beginning to wonder if I wasn't right in my first assumption after all.' His long fingers bridged the distance between them and she gave a tiny, tell-tale start as he touched her

27

chin, lifting it a little so that she was forced to look straight into those bottomless blue eyes. 'Suppose I did what Elizabeth and Janet obviously want and offered to marry you, Faith Bridges? Would you stay then?'

It was so long since anyone had made her blush — really blush — that she couldn't be sure that that was what she was doing, but the tingle that tormented Faith's cheekbones seemed horribly familiar. She swallowed, tried to remember that she was *renowned* for level-headedness. 'Are you really *that* desperate?' she asked, congratulating herself for retaining her cool manner under pressure.

'Not yet.' She had expected a lopsided grin, an admission of defeat. Disconcertingly, Harry March was not smiling. 'But come back in a couple of days and who can tell?'

Faith felt herself slipping under the spell of the man her aunt had described as irresistible. It was a challenge. She could resist — she'd prove it.

'I'm sorry, Mr March, but since you're not my type and I'm already spoken for you'll have to think of something else. But, just in case you're still not convinced, I'll tell you why I came galloping post-haste to your rescue — ' Aunt Janet won't like it, her subconscious intervened hastily.

Harry March glanced at Mac. 'This should be interesting.'

Faith consigned her subconscious to the devil. Aunt Janet was safely tucked up in her hospital bed, and it wouldn't do this smooth manipulator of women any harm at all to know just how far people were prepared to go to help him for precious little thanks.

'My aunt received your cry for help just before I arrived to take her into hospital for a hip replacement,' she informed him, a touch recklessly for someone *renowned* for her level-headedness. 'In fact,' she continued, enthusiastically warming to her subject, 'she threatened to miss her operation and come herself if I didn't promise to come and find out exactly what the crisis was and do what I could to help. And, since she's waited three years for that operation, Mr March, I promised.'

2

'Blackmailed you, did she?'

'Certainly not!' Faith declared, ignoring the fact that she had used the same word.

Harry March ignored her disavowal. 'Still, a promise is a promise,' he said, 'even when apparently extracted under duress.' The familiar phrase, drummed into her by her aunt since she was knee-high to a gnat, sounded odd coming from him, and yet Janet Bridges had looked after him until he'd gone away to school. He would certainly be as well versed in her aunt's virtuous homilies as she was and, like her aunt, he was apparently quite capable of a little blackmail on his own account.

'I've kept my promise, Mr March.'

'To the letter and not an inch beyond it,' he retaliated sharply, mixing metaphors to considerable effect and making her feel just a little mean-hearted. She hadn't been sure what reaction her revelation would provoke — irritation, perhaps, that something like an arthritic hip should be allowed to interfere with his concerns — but the anger that expressed itself upon the man's features was unexpected. 'Three years? She's been waiting three years for her operation? Good grief, why on earth didn't she tell me?' he demanded. 'She knew I'd have paid for private treatment for her, but she's never even hinted . . . ' He paused. 'You're right, of course. It's two years or more since I last saw her. I should have realised that something was wrong when she kept putting me off. Damn!'

'My father and I did offer to pay for private treatment for her.' Could it be that she was trying to rehabilitate herself in this man's eyes? 'She wouldn't hear of it. Said it would be queue-jumping.'

'That's predictable, I suppose.' They exchanged a look that acknowledged

Janet Bridges' unshakable will. 'When is she having her operation?'

'Tomorrow morning,' Faith said, slightly mollified by this totally unexpected show of concern.

'Where?'

She told him.

'Well, at least I can get her a private room. The hospital can think up some reason for moving her. And I'll send her some roses from the garden. They have more scent than those dreadful hothouse things they sell in florists.'

'I don't know about the room, but she'd love the roses. She's very . . . fond of you.' Then, slightly embarrassed by such a statement, she quickly continued. 'I could take them back with me if you like,' Faith offered.

'It's a little late to be picking flowers, Miss Bridges, and far too late for you to drive all the way back to London tonight. And to be honest I'd feel a lot happier if you would at least stay until a proper nanny can be despatched to take your place. Just in case . . . ' He gestured towards the sleeping child and smiled.

The gesture was so graceful, the smile of such self-deprecating charm, so utterly different from that automatic knock-'em-dead smile he had used earlier that Faith found herself not only ignoring the alarm bells ringing frantically in her head but responding helplessly, as women had been doing since he had first discovered his power to bend them to his will when he had been little more than a babe-in-arms himself.

Besides, it wasn't the smile that moved her, she told herself foolishly. She had been planning to stop at the first hotel she passed on the way home and stay the night. It would be idiotic to refuse Harry March's hospitality just because he thought he was getting his own way. After all, she knew better.

And if she stayed to see the temporary nanny in place then she could be absolutely easy in her mind that she had carried out her promise to her aunt. That remark about keeping her promise 'to the letter' had hurt more than she would ever admit. And, as Harry March had reminded her, a promise was a promise, even when extracted under duress. She could almost hear Aunt Janet saying the words.

What about your promise not to tell Harry March that she was in hospital? her conscience prompted, rather unkindly. Just because you wanted to make him feel bad.

Guiltily, she glanced down at the sleeping baby. 'Well, if I'm staying, I suppose the least I can do is put Ben to bed,' she said. 'Then I can make a few telephone calls and organise someone who knows what they're doing to help you out.'

'That's very kind of you, Miss Bridges,' Harry said, taking her arm with grave courtesy, his long, graceful fingers curving beneath her elbow, cool against her skin. 'I'll show you the way, shall I? I'm sure you'd like to change out of that damp blouse. And I can introduce you to Alice if she's still awake,' he added.

'Alice?' Faith felt her stomach contract with alarm.

'Ben's sister. She's four. Well, very nearly five.'

Another child! Her stomach had been right. Faith, despite the damp patch on her shoulder and a rapidly developing ache in her arm from the unaccustomed weight of the baby, had started to feel in control of the situation. Now she gave an inward groan. The sooner she got away from Wickham Ash the better. 'Mac, could you rustle up something special for dinner, since I have a guest?'

Faith saw Mac's face finally twist into something that might have been a smile. But whether it was because he was genuinely pleased she was staying or was simply amused at the ease with which Harry March had got his own way, she couldn't be quite sure. It didn't worry her much either way because, whatever happened, she would be leaving first thing in the morning.

'Why has your sister left the children with you?' she asked, drawing Harry out of some deep thought.

'Hmm? Oh, she was staying here while her husband was in the States on business. He's been in a road accident so she's gone rushing off to mop his fevered brow.'

'Is he badly hurt?'

'No, but you know how women love to worry.'

'What ever would men do if women didn't worry about them?' she asked, just a touch sharply.

'Have a quiet life?' he offered.

''A quiet life'? Nothing that Aunt Janet ever told me about you suggested that you wanted that, Mr March.'

'Harry, please,' he said, turning sharply to look down at her as if wondering exactly what Janet Bridges had been saying about him. She hoped, sincerely, that he wouldn't ask. ''Mr March' makes me feel positively geriatric.'

She doubted that. 'Mac calls you sir,' she pointed out. 'Surely that's far worse?'

'Mac was my sergeant when I was in the army and he's somewhat set in his ways. Despite strenuous efforts to get him to call me Harry, I haven't yet been able to break him of the habit. But I'm working on it.'

'Oh, I see. And is he looking for a quiet life too?' Faith asked as they reached the top of the stairs.

The ear-splitting scream that rent the air rendered any answer redundant and Harry March abruptly relinquished his hold upon her elbow to sprint awkwardly along the gallery as a small, dark-haired figure dressed in a long white nightgown appeared from one of the doorways.

'Alice? What is it, kitten?' He swung the child up into his arms and tucked her against his shoulder.

'I had a bad dream, Uncle Harry,' Alice said pathetically, wrapping her arms about Harry's neck and pressing her cheek against his darker skin. 'I want my mummy.'

'I know you do, darling. She'll be home soon with Daddy,' he murmured soothingly, but Alice had already spotted Faith, and, bad dream apparently forgotten, she pointed dramatically. 'Who's she?' she demanded.

Faith, who had suffered from bad dreams after her mother had been killed in a road accident, might not have known much about children but she recognised a fake nightmare when she saw one. The child was undoubtedly missing her mother, but Faith could certainly do Harry the favour of letting Alice know that not all adults were as gullible as doting uncles. 'My name's Faith,' she said briskly, heading for the room from which the child had appeared. 'I used to have bad dreams too. Would you like me to tell you about them?'

'Is that a good idea?' Harry intervened sharply.

'Oh, yes,' Faith said, with every appearance of confidence. 'If I show her how it should be done she'll be much more convincing next time,' she added matter-of-factly, holding out her free hand to the child. Alice clung tightly to her uncle. Faith shrugged. 'You see, Alice, if you splash your nightdress with water,' she said encouragingly, 'and then sort of twist it all round you like this . . . ' She shifted Ben slightly to demonstrate with her skirt. The child's eyes lit up and Faith knew she had been right. 'It's cold and not very comfortable but it really frightens the grown-ups — '

'What kind of nanny are you?' Harry demanded, horrified, following her to the door.

She glanced up at him. 'I told you, Mr March, I'm not any kind of a nanny. I'm a banker.'

His dark brows drew together, disparagingly. 'You obviously relish your work. What do you do to the poor souls who run up an overdraft? Lock them in the coal cellar until they promise to be good?'

'No, I advise the bank and its clients on ethical investments. However, if your bank has nothing better than coal to keep in its cellar, Mr March, I would seriously recommend changing to a different establishment. But perhaps you're right.' She offered him the baby. 'Perhaps you should take care of the children yourself while I get back to London. All this fresh air seems to be going to my head.' Ben, who had slept through the commotion, now stirred and whimpered.

'On the contrary, you seem to have everything well under control.' He declined to retrieve his nephew and she settled him back under her chin, crooning gently to him so that the baby frown disappeared from his tiny brow. She glanced up.

'Then maybe you should go and have that drink you were promising yourself?'

Alice, who had continued to stare at Faith from the safety of her uncle's arms for a moment, turned to Harry.

'It's all right, Uncle Harry, you can go away now,' she said imperiously. '*She* can put me to bed.'

'Well, I'll be damned!'

'Mummy said you weren't to use that word in front of me,' Alice admonished him severely, before wriggling free and dropping to the floor. She took Faith's hand, smiling up at her brightly. 'Come on,' she ordered. 'It's this way.'

'It seems you have your answer, Faith Bridges. Out of the mouths of babes and sucklings . . . ' And an infuriatingly smug little smile tugged at the corner of Harry's mouth.

Faith said nothing, contenting herself with granting him the kind of look that she normally reserved for spiders in the bath before smiling down at Alice. 'Will you help me put Ben to bed first?' she asked. 'I haven't a clue where anything is.'

'I'll show you,' Alice said. 'You can go now, Uncle Harry.' She shooed him away.

But Harry, it seemed, was in no great

hurry to depart, and leant against the door as Faith settled Ben into his cot, fussed around by Alice, who offered advice with all the seriousness of an old wife.

'You seem to know an awful lot about babies, Alice,' Faith said.

'I help my mummy all the time. I'm five next week,' she said confidingly, then added artlessly, 'How old are you?'

Faith probably imagined a chuckle from the door. She had never made a fuss about her age, but she rather wished Harry March had taken himself off, as instructed by his niece. She gritted her teeth and said, 'Twenty-five.'

'That's old,' Alice replied sympathetically, before helpfully adding, 'But Uncle Harry's much older than that. He's older than mummy and she was twenty-eight when it was her birthday.'

'Oh, I know all about your Uncle Harry,' Faith informed the child. 'My aunt Janet was his nanny and she told me all about him. Did you know that he was a very naughty little boy?'

Alice peered around Faith at Harry, clearly finding it difficult to believe that he had ever been a little boy. 'How naughty?' she asked.

'Oh, he put frogs in her bed and glued her shoes to the floor, and once, when he was very bad and was told to stay in his room, he climbed out of the window and fell and broke his leg.'

'I didn't fall. The drainpipe broke,' Harry corrected her.

She turned to face him. 'I see. The drainpipe broke and then you fell and broke your leg.' She knew her aunt had blamed herself for the accident and that made her angry. It must surely have been plain to anyone not besotted with the boy that he was spoilt and reckless and deserved every minute of the long, hot summer he had spent stuck in a plaster cast? Her eyes said it all. She was disconcerted to discover that his own acknowledged as much and, embarrassed, she turned back to Alice. 'Come along, back into bed with you,' she said.

But Alice, eyes wide, wanted to know more. 'Is that why you walk lopsy, Uncle Harry?' she asked. 'Does your leg still hurt?'

Very conscious of Harry's tall figure leaning against the doorpost, eyes narrowed as he watched her, Faith had decided to retaliate a little, pay him back for his less than gracious reception of her when she had put herself out to help him. But now the words turned sour in her mouth and she started guiltily as he swept past her and picked up the child, carrying her across to her bed. 'No, sweetheart. When I climbed out of the window it was the other leg that was broken.'

The child still wasn't satisfied. 'Well, how did you hurt that leg?' she demanded, pointing to the one that he limped on.

'Doing something a lot more danger-ous than climbing out of a first-floor window. Although *that* was a very stupid thing to do,' he added, throwing a swift glance at Faith, demanding instant backup.

'Very stupid,' Faith agreed quickly. 'Only a boy would ever do anything so silly. A girl would have used her brains . . . '

A dangerous light sparked in Harry's dark eyes before his face quite suddenly dissolved into a grin. 'Whereas it's an acknowledged fact that boys don't have any,' he finished for her. 'Hop into bed, Alice, and I'll read you a story.'

'I want *Faith* to tell me a story.'

'I think Faith has told enough stories for one evening,' Harry said pointedly. 'Settle down now, while I show her where her room is, and then I'll come back and read to you.'

Her lower lip trembled and for a moment rebellion threatened. 'Faith put Ben to bed. I want her to put me to bed too.'

'But I didn't tell him a story,' Faith pointed out, tucking the covers around her. 'Uncle Harry did that,' she added, her fingers crossed behind her.

This seemed to mollify the child a little. 'You'll come back and kiss me g'night won't you, Faith?' she asked sweetly.

'Yes, Alice, I'll come back,' Faith promised, from the doorway.

'This is your room,' Harry said, leading the way along the corridor to the next room and throwing open the door for her. Faith, however, lingered before taking refuge.

'I'm really sorry. It was very stupid of me to have told her that you climbed out of the window, but I did warn you. I'm just not used to dealing with children.'

'A minor slip. You're doing pretty well so far,' he conceded magnanimously. 'She had me fooled.'

'I guess it takes experience to spot a fake.'

'Experience?'

'I suffered from bad dreams after my mother was killed by a car outside our home,' she explained reluctantly.

He nodded but wasn't crass enough to say that he was sorry. 'I see. Well, in that case I'm sure that if Janet gave you a blow-by-blow description of the reason I walk as if my leg hurts you'll keep it to yourself.'

'She didn't,' she said quickly. 'It's just that when I was a little girl she used to tell me about the things the children she cared for got up to. I'm afraid you featured rather heavily.'

'I was a bit of a handful and I gave her a very hard time, but she was the nearest thing I ever had to a proper mother. I've done my best to make it up to her since. However, now you've done your best to put me firmly in my Bath chair perhaps you'd prefer to call me Mr March after all.'

'I don't think so.' She didn't think he would prefer it either. 'But when I was seven, you were fifteen, a vastly grand and distant figure performing heroic feats on the sports field of your public school.'

He pulled a face. 'A legend in my own lifetime, no doubt.' Almost. But she wasn't about to boost his ego by telling him of the scrapbook her aunt kept of his exploits — winning a rowing blue for his university, laughing his way across the pages of the society magazines, on the polo field or at some charity ball, always with a beautiful girl on his arm, always with a glass of champagne in his hand. 'How things change,' he added, a touch bitterly, as he crossed the bedroom and threw open a door concealed in the dark panelling. 'You have your own bathroom. Is there anything you need?' he asked, turning to her.

She shook her head. 'No, thanks. I'll just go and get my overnight bag from the car.'

He held out his hand. 'Give me your keys and I'll fetch it for you.'

'There's really no need. I'm quite capable of carrying a small bag . . . '

'So am I, despite the limp.' He snapped his fingers impatiently.

'I didn't mean that . . . ' She swallowed. 'And besides, the keys are in my shoulder bag, downstairs. I can manage, really; it's not in the least bit

49

heavy and Alice is waiting for you . . . '
She was babbling, she realised with
disbelief. Faith Bridges — efficient,
unemotional, unflappable under pressure — was *babbling*.

Harry appeared not to notice, or
maybe women were always reduced to
babbling in his presence. The man
should have a health warning printed
across that scarred and glowering
forehead of his in letters an inch high,
she thought as he finally shrugged and
turned away. 'Please yourself. Come
down and have a drink when you're
done. I'll be in the library.'

Back in her bedroom, with the door
safely closed against the disconcerting
masculine presence in the house, she at
least managed a wry grin as she stood
in front of the dressing table. Doe-eyed
blonde indeed, she thought, unfasten-
ing the tortoiseshell clip that held her
long, thick hair at the nape of her neck
and feathering the strands out with her
fingers.

Her eyes were large enough, she

acknowledged, but of a most ordinary brown and, as for her hair — well, she had no illusions about that. When she had been about fifteen she had made the mistake of enquiring casually of her father if her hair could be classed as blonde.

'Your hair is mouse, my girl,' he'd informed her in his matter-of-fact way, peering at her over the top of his newspaper. 'Cheerful mouse, if you like, but the only way you'll ever be a blonde is out of a bottle.'

So she had scoured the enticing shelves of a high-street chemist, purchasing a bottle of hair colouring which in the secrecy of the bathroom had turned her hair bright guinea-gold. Her father had never said a word during the long months it had taken to grow out. Presumably he'd thought that having to live with the ghastly colour was lesson enough.

And after Michael's desertion he had been equally matter-of-fact. 'Count your blessings. Work hard and use your spare time in looking for ways to help other people instead of feeling sorry for yourself.' An undemonstrative man, he had done this himself after the crushing blow of his wife's death. It was what he preached from his pulpit every Sunday. She took his advice, but how she had longed for him, just once, to take her into his arms and simply hug her.

Faith sat on the edge of the bed. She hadn't thought about Michael for a long time. Not really thought about him. Or the wild, giddy romance that had swept her off her feet so that she hadn't known what day of the week it was, hadn't cared about her place at university, hadn't cared about anything but the joy of being in love, the life they were going to have together and the dozens and dozens of children . . . Her heart snagged on the thought and she backed away from it.

She had blotted him out of her mind with the same relentless determination with which she had applied herself to her career. She had dumped him, and all the painful emotions that she associated with him, with his ring, in the river. And she had promised herself, Never again. And now Harry March, who had done the same to his beautiful Clementine, had dredged all those feelings up again just as she had her life organised, settled . . .

'Faith!' Alice, impatient for her kiss, called out, interrupting the disquieting thoughts.

Pulling herself together, she went back to the nursery. Alice was waiting for her, sitting up, determined not to fall asleep before she had claimed her kiss.

'You were so long!' she complained as Faith sat on the bed beside her.

'Sorry. I'm not used to looking after little girls.'

'Will you stay with me until my mummy comes back, Faith?'

'I'll be here when you wake up tomorrow, Alice,' she promised, hating herself for not being able just to say yes to such trusting innocence. But it just wasn't possible.

'Will Mummy be home then?' the child persisted.

'I think you'd better ask Uncle Harry about that,' she said. 'Time to go to sleep now.' She kissed the child, settled her down under the covers, tidied away her story books and checked on Ben. By the time she had done that, Alice was asleep. She turned off the overhead light, leaving the soft glow of the nursery lamp throwing a pink blush onto the curve of the child's cheek.

Julian, thoughtful, deeply caring, was firm in his belief that the world already had enough children and that he would not add to the planet's burden. It had seemed so sensible, written in his small, neat handwriting, using the refillable fountain pen and the recycled paper he had asked her to send him. Not a sacrifice at all. But, looking at the two sleeping infants, she wondered briefly what sense had to do with the soft touch of a baby's breath against your cheek, the trusting grip of his fingers wrapped tightly about one of your own.

That was all she allowed herself to wonder before she pulled the door halfway closed and beat a retreat to her own room to take a quick, invigorating shower.

She changed into a pair of softly pleated moss-coloured trousers in a fabric rich enough for the evening and a shirt in the palest primrose silk. She added just a touch of make-up to skin honeyed by weekend walks with her father alongside the river and left her long, straight hair loose about her shoulders.

Harry was standing at the window when she walked through the library door and he turned as he heard her. 'All peaceful?' he asked, a smile lining his cheeks.

This older, darker Harry March was, she decided, far more dangerously handsome, for all his scars, than ever the young Harry March had been. He had been too perfect, too beautiful and the jealous gods had exacted their revenge. Now, with the evening light slanting in through the mullioned windows throwing his features into sharp contrast, hollowing his cheeks, sharpening the angles of his face, and with his white open-necked shirt billowing loosely above the tightly stretched fabric of his jeans, he had all the appearance of a battle-hardened buccaneer. He lacked only the piratical glint of gold at one ear, she thought, then caught herself. Sensible women, *level-headed* women, avoided pirates.

'All peaceful,' she replied. At least in the nursery. Her heart had gone racketing off on some mad roller-coaster ride the moment he had smiled at her. 'But Alice wants to know when her mummy is coming home.'

'I can't tell her what I don't know.' He lifted his shoulders in a resigned shrug. 'Faith, I've had Janet on the telephone.'

'She said she'd ring to make sure I arrived in one piece.' Her aunt did not approve of her racy little sports car. Neither did Julian, come to that. He firmly believed that everyone not using a bicycle should be using public transport. The moment he came home she would have to surrender her car and buy a season ticket for the bus. And quite right too. 'Is she all right?'

He pulled a face. 'There's certainly nothing wrong with her voice. When I told her you couldn't stay she threatened to discharge herself from hospital and come straight down here.'

'You told her I wasn't staying?' Faith demanded. 'Of all the idiotic, stupid . . . ' Words failed her as Harry's eyebrows hit the ceiling.

'I'm so sorry,' he said, with just enough irony so that she would know he wasn't a bit sorry. 'I didn't realise that it was a state secret.'

'It isn't, but I would have thought that even you could have foreseen the consequences of telling her. Or was that the reason you told her? Were you going in for a little emotional blackmail on your own behalf, Harry March?'

'Only the guilty are susceptible to

blackmail, Faith.' Guilty! The nerve of the man! Yet although his eyes were expressionless she sensed a deep anger inside him. Well, he had no right to be angry and she was damned if she would explain why she couldn't stay. It was none of his business.

'I would have gone to see her the minute I got back,' she said frostily, refusing to allow herself to be browbeaten by the man. 'By then she would have had her operation.' He was unmoved. 'Please, Harry, she can't possibly come here. You've got to stop her, whatever it takes. She finds it hard enough to cope just with looking after herself.'

'And you've just let her get on with it?'

'She's a stubborn woman. I told you that we offered to pay for the operation but she wouldn't — ' His exclamation of disgust infuriated her. 'Well, what would you have done? Knocked her out with your famous killer charm and performed surgery yourself with your trusty cutlass?' No, no, that was pirates . . . 'She seems to think you can walk on water so maybe a magic wand would have done the trick . . . ' She stopped abruptly. Mixing metaphors was apparently catching.

'I don't have a magic wand, or a cutlass. But I certainly wouldn't have tiptoed around her in case I hurt her feelings,' he said curtly. 'I'd have told her the truth in words she would have understood.'

'Oh, really. This I have got to hear,' she declared, inviting him to demonstrate his technique.

His mouth twisted in something that sketched at a grin. 'I would have told her that she was behaving like a spoilt five-year-old who was scared of the dentist.'

Faith's eyes widened at the very idea of telling her formidable aunt anything of the kind. 'You anticipated *surviving* this meeting?'

The grin disappeared. 'Janet and I understand one another. She would have been honest enough to recognise the truth when she was forced to look it in the face. Just because she's a tough old bird it doesn't mean that she isn't frightened witless at the thought of surgery.' He allowed a gleam to brighten the darkness of his eyes. 'Whatever made you think I had a cutlass?'

She ignored the question. 'Aunt Janet? Frightened?' The same Aunt Janet who for more than thirty years had inspired children with the courage to face all the pains, small and large, that life threw at them, from a grazed knee to a broken leg? The idea was crazy.

'Everyone's frightened of anaesthetic,' he said darkly. 'It's surrendering yourself to the unknown . . . ' He stared into his glass. Faith, who had never experienced the terror for herself, realised that he had, and she didn't argue, although he waited, clearly expecting some response. When none came he looked up. 'She's obviously been doing everything she can to put

60

off the evil day and right now you're playing into her hands, Faith.'

'Me!'

'Yes, you, Miss Faith Bridges, renowned for your level-headedness. Unless you get on the telephone and take away the one excuse left to her. And if you think that I'm using emotional blackmail I can live with that.'

Faith found it hard to meet those eyes. 'No,' she said finally. 'You obviously just want what's best for her as well.' She glanced around. 'So where's the telephone?'

'I'll show you.' He wheeled away from the window and led the way across the hall to a small room tucked away beneath the stairs. The contrast between the world of oak panelling and dust motes dancing in the last shafts of sunlight streaming in through mullioned windows and this room could not have been more striking.

She had expected a venerable antique desk with a Georgian silver inkstand. Instead the windowless room was packed with dull grey metal housing an array of computer screens and a communications centre that wouldn't have disgraced the bank where until recently she'd spent her working hours.

Harry touched a button and the telephone number of Janet's hospital appeared on the nearest screen. He touched another and it began to dial. He lifted a telephone receiver and offered it to Faith. 'She should have been moved to a private room by now. Don't tell her that I arranged it.'

'She's not stupid, Harry.'

He paused and turned in the doorway. 'No. And neither are you. I'm sure you know exactly what to say to keep her where she is. But if she gives you any trouble just remind her what she said to me in similar circumstances.'

'What was that?'

'She knows.' And with that he closed the door behind him, leaving her alone.

The telephone in Janet's room rang for so long that she was beginning to wonder if her aunt had already put her threat into action and left the hospital.

'Hello? Who's there?'

The familiar voice with its sharp query sent relief flooding through her. 'Aunt Janet, it's Faith. Harry said you rang earlier.'

'Yes, I did. And you can tell him that if he thinks I'm going to stay in a private room with no one to gossip to he's got another think coming. It's no good that young nurse saying that I need to be quiet before my operation; I know he's behind it. Tell him I said so.'

Faith grinned helplessly. 'I'll tell him.'

'On second thought, don't bother. I'll tell him myself when I see him. Are those children of Elizabeth's all right?'

'Fine. Tucked up in bed. So much for your promise that there would be no babies.'

'Well, you wouldn't have gone, would you?' She didn't wait for a reply. 'Anyway, you needn't bother your head about them after tomorrow. The minute I can find my clothes, I'll be out of here. I've already called a taxi.'

3

'Then cancel it!' Faith held her breath, crossed her fingers and, hoping that Harry March was right, launched her attack. 'I can't believe you're being such a baby about a perfectly simple operation, Janet Bridges. If it was one of us you wouldn't stand for this kind of nonsense. You'll be a new woman once it's over.'

'I don't know what you're talking about.' Only someone who knew her well would have detected the tiny tremor of uncertainty in the woman's voice.

'You know perfectly well what I'm talking about, Aunt Janet.' Then, more gently, she added, 'It's quite normal to be scared, you know. Nothing to be ashamed of.' She paused. 'Harry sent you a message.'

'Humph.' Then Janet asked irritably,

'Well, what is it?'

'He said to remind you of what you said to him once. In similar circumstances.'

There was a long pause. 'Faith?'

'Aunt Janet?'

'I'm sorry I didn't tell you the reason Harry needed help, but will you promise me something?'

'Only if you promise me that you'll stay in that hospital bed.' She was learning fast.

'If I do, will you stay with Harry?' But not fast enough, apparently. 'Just until he can find someone to take my place.'

Faith let out a long sigh of relief. She had expected her aunt to extract a promise to stay until their mother returned. She had already agreed to stay until the next day and a replacement would be on the way the moment the agencies opened in the morning. 'No one could ever take your place, Aunt Janet,' she said, a little hoarsely as her throat tightened. She cleared it. 'I can't think why you ever imagined I was suitable in the first place.'

'I couldn't think of anyone else at such short notice.'

'Oh, thanks.'

Janet Bridges chuckled. 'You'll manage.'

'Yes, I suppose I will. And I promise that I'll stay until Harry finds a replacement for me.' She paused. 'I'll be thinking of you tomorrow. Dad said he would come in first thing to see you, before you go to Theatre . . . It'll be all right . . . '

'Yes, dear, I know. And thank you.'

Harry looked up from the drinks tray as she let herself into the library. 'Everything settled? You were rather a long time.'

'I thought I'd better look in on the children. They're both fast asleep.'

'It happens occasionally. Drink?'

She would have liked a very large drink but she shook her head. 'Just a tonic water since I'm on duty.' He raised an eyebrow but said nothing as he poured it for her. She gave an awkward little shrug. 'I promised to stay until you found someone else to look after the children.'

He raised one dark brow as he handed her the glass. 'More blackmail?'

'No. I'd already agreed to stay tonight. It was your message that did the trick. She went very quiet.' The tonic water fizzed sharply against her tongue as she took a sip and braved the slightly puzzled expression that crossed his face, narrowed his eyes. 'What did she say to you, Harry?'

'She reminded me, when I needed it most, that pride feels no pain.' Faith's eyes instinctively flew to his leg, and she wondered just what had happened to the glad-foot lad of her aunt's stories. What had smashed his leg and ripped across the smooth, broad forehead? Her swift glance was intercepted and his mouth twisted in a provocative little smile. 'There's more than one kind of pain, Faith.' He downed his whisky and turned away to refill his glass. 'Do you want to make any more calls? I imagine your boyfriend must be wondering what's become of you.'

'Boyfriend?' she repeated blankly.

He looked up. 'You said you were spoken for. Perhaps I'm old-fashioned, but I assumed it must be a man.'

'Of course it's a man!' Faith could feel the heat rushing to her face and realised to her horror that she was blushing again. Not cool. Not cool enough by half. 'His name is Julian,' she said, with as much chill as she could muster, but she never referred to him as her *boyfriend*. That word suggested all kinds of crazy things that had nothing to do with their mature and sensible relationship. 'Julian Fellowes. But I can't telephone him. He's out of the country at the moment.'

Harry shrugged. 'I'm not about to throw a faint if you want to call Saudi Arabia or Hong Kong or somewhere equally remote.'

Remote. He thought Hong Kong was remote? She was tempted to tell him exactly where Julian was at this very moment and wipe that provoking expression straight off his face. She was tempted, but she resisted, certain that he would make some irritating remark that would make her forget all about being level-headed and lose her temper. He was already overloading her emotional circuits with irrational and unexpected feelings that she had no desire to explore further.

'Thank you, Harry,' she said calmly. Too calmly. A dangerous symptom, given the provocation. 'But it isn't that easy to get in touch. And since he won't know I'm not at home it really doesn't matter.'

'You don't live together, then?'

She made a pretence of being thoroughly shocked. 'Please! I'm the daughter of a clergyman.' His look was speculative and she suddenly wished that she had stuck to a simple no. Intent upon squashing any further reference to the matter, she quickly continued. 'Look, I know one or two people who have nannies; perhaps I'd better go and call them to ask for advice about how to find someone for you.'

'There's no rush.' *No rush?* Did he think that she would be able to conjure up the perfect nanny at the drop of a hat? Or was he simply going out of his way to make her angry? She had told him that it was a matter of the utmost urgency that she get back to London. 'You can at least finish your drink.' His mouth twisted into an irritating little smile. It was almost as if he knew what she was thinking and enjoyed making her rise to his bait.

Faith glanced down at the glass in her hand. It was tall and slender, filled with ice and lemon and the sharp fizz of tonic water that made it hard to swallow quickly. Besides, gulping it down would betray her eagerness to be out of the room, out of Harry March's life. She was sure that would amuse him and she couldn't think why. She only knew that she didn't want to be an object of this man's amusement.

Keeping her feelings firmly under control, she sipped her drink slowly and decided to deal with the question of a nanny as if it were simply one of the many problems that had passed across her desk in the course of a working day. Efficiently, objectively, smoothly and without a trace of emotion. 'What kind of woman are you looking for, since you're going to have to live with her?'

Sure that he had her at his beck and call until she could find a suitable replacement, his slow, trawling look as he covered the distance from her ankles to her chin was designed to provoke. 'Frankly, my dear, I'm more than happy with the woman I've got. You're the one who's being difficult.'

'I am not! I told you . . . ' So much for her buttoned-up emotions. She began again. 'I have things to do. Things that won't wait.'

'What things?'

His eyes sparkled as he goaded her. Had she thought they were cornflower-blue? Not cornflower. Darker. Much darker than that. Faith's grasp tight-ened on the glass and she tried again to take control of the situation. She usually found it so easy, but Harry March refused to play by the rules. 'It would be a help if I knew how long you are likely to need someone,' she continued briskly.

'I'm sure it would. Let's see now . . . ' His smile taunted her, as if he wanted her to know that he could read her deepest thoughts. 'I thought a week, but in your case I'm sure I could be persuaded to spin it out a little longer — '

'Dinner's ready.' Mac's timely interruption saved her from making an absolute idiot of herself and she turned to him gratefully. 'I've laid a table out in the garden, miss, as it's so warm this evening.'

'In the garden? But what about the children? I won't hear them if we're outside,' Faith said anxiously, turning to Harry, glad of something ordinary, something practical to concentrate her mind.

Harry took a small device from his pocket and switched it on before placing it in her hand and closing her fingers about it. It was warm from the heat of his body. That and the unexpected touch of his hand wrapped about hers sent a tiny frisson of excitement rippling across her skin, and she gave a little shiver.

Harry frowned. 'Are you cold? We can eat inside — '

'No,' she said, too quickly. 'Um . . . just a little tired, perhaps. It's been a long day and I had a late night — '

'A late night? And Julian away?' He made a small tutting sound and his face positively begged to be slapped.

'With the prospectus of a company that wants to be recommended as ethical,' she continued, as if he hadn't interrupted.

'What a waste.'

'No, as a matter of fact,' she returned sharply. She could have left it for her successor to wrap up, but she had known that underneath all the pious platitudes of the directors there had been something not quite right. It had taken a lot of digging and a great deal of time to uncover the abuse of child labour, but not one moment, in her opinion, had been wasted. She had delivered her report to the bank on the way to pick up Janet. 'I turned them down.'

'Politely, I hope,' he murmured, raising one thoughtful brow the merest fraction, and she wondered, uneasily, what her face had shown. She could normally disguise her feelings, but nothing about the day had been normal. Harry didn't wait for her response, simply tapping the small device he had placed in her hand. 'This is a baby alarm. If you turn it up sufficiently, you will be able to hear Alice and Ben breathing.' Still cupping her hand in his, he demonstrated, and she could clearly hear two sets of breathing. 'You'll know if one of them so much as hiccups. It's good for half a mile.'

'An awful lot could happen in the time it took me to cover half a mile,' she said.

He grinned, unexpectedly revealing a flash of the young Harry. 'A trifle over-designed, perhaps, but then I adapted it from a listening device used by the intelligence services.'

'You should market it,' she advised.

'And have husbands listening in on their wives, bosses on their employees and everyone listening in on their neighbours? I might make a fortune, but would it be . . . *ethical*?' She glared at him. 'Shall we go outside?'

He removed his hand from hers and placed it instead at the small of her back. It was enough to send her rocketing obediently through the open door.

'Outside' turned out to be a small walled garden reached through a large, ornate and rather daunting dining room of the kind Faith had seen in houses open to the public and which was hardly the ideal venue for an intimate dinner for two.

She snatched back that dangerous thought and stuffed it down behind the sofa cushions of her mind as she stepped through the French windows. She was marrying Julian in three weeks' time. She had absolutely no business thinking about intimate dinners with Harry March. Then the enchantment of the small garden enveloped her.

The walls were eight or nine feet high and built of the same warm stone as the house — stone that had weathered softly and was now covered by eager, scrambling roses woven with honeysuckle that scented the still evening air. The stone-flagged floor was liberally furnished with tubs of pink geraniums and ivies, and the tiny leaves of lemon thyme burgeoned from the cracks in the paving stones, to be crushed beneath their feet as they walked across to the white wrought-iron table set in the corner to catch the last heat from the sun.

'Someone is an inspired gardener,' Faith said as Harry pulled back one of the chairs for her and his hand brushed against her shoulder. Gardening, like the weather, was a safe, neutral subject of conversation.

He looked around him as if he hadn't noticed its charms before and Faith realised how stupid she had been. She had been thinking how much her father would have loved a walled garden in which to grow his tenderest treasures. But Harry March clearly never had to bother with anything as humble as gardening. He simply paid someone to do it for him, the way his mother and other women like her had paid Aunt Janet to bring up their children — by the hour.

He had been born to privilege, with servants and a nanny to attend to every need, horses, dogs, and acres of countryside to roam without ever leaving his own land. When he had grown older there had been a glamorous regiment to join and the daughter of another, equally well-endowed family to fall at his feet — a beautiful girl with shiny fair hair and huge bright eyes fixed adoringly on him in the photo of when their engagement had been announced in one of the society magazines that her aunt was addicted to.

As she turned from her contemplation of the flowers and met the questioning blue eyes of the man opposite her she felt a little quiver of alarm ripple her spine. There was something probing about the look and for a moment she wondered if she had fallen into the trap, was looking at him in the same besotted manner as Clementine . . .

She came rapidly back to earth. She'd had quite enough of men who asked girls to marry them and then changed their minds. 'Where's Mac? Isn't he eating with us?'

'Mac prefers the kitchen.' He smiled slightly, as if aware that Mac would have provided a buffer between them, amused that she felt the need of it. 'But he's within shouting distance. If you should feel threatened.'

'Threatened?' Her tongue trembled

slightly on the word. 'Why on earth should I feel threatened?'

'I have no idea, but you seem somewhat nervous. You're quite safe, you know. I'm not in the habit of pestering the hired help.'

'What?' Her laugh sounded forced even to her own ears. 'Never had a tumble in the hayloft with a scullery maid?' Ah, but that wouldn't be pestering. What scullery maid could have resisted the overtures of the youthful Harry March? He didn't bother to dignify this with a reply but continued to regard her with eyes creased in gentle irony, as if he knew precisely what she was thinking. She stiffened. 'Besides, I'm not hired. I'm doing you a favour.'

His smile deepened. 'So you are, and if you had not made a point of informing me that you are already spoken for, Faith Bridges, I might just have taken that as an invitation.' He ignored her enraged gasp. 'Tell me about this Julian Fellowes. I believe you said he was overseas?'

'Yes, I believe I did.' She stuck her fork in the trout, managed a tiny morsel. 'This is delicious,' she said.

'Tell Mac. He does it all himself. Including the fishing.'

'And what do *you* do?' Her tone left him in no doubt of her suspicion that he did very little indeed.

'Me?' His eyes glinted wickedly. 'Apart from teasing young women who take themselves far too seriously?' He didn't wait for a reply. 'I manage to keep myself amused. I like to play around with electronics.'

'Like the baby alarm?'

'It's one of my toys,' he confirmed. 'Why don't you have a glass of this wine?' he said, filling her glass. 'Elizabeth certainly would if she were here.'

Faith ignored the wine. 'When did you say she'd be back?'

'I didn't. It all depends on John, her husband, but I'll call her later; maybe she'll be able to give me some idea.' He continued to regard her thoughtfully. 'Is he a missionary?'

'I beg your pardon?'

'Julian Fellowes. You said you are the daughter of a clergyman. I thought perhaps you had been snapped up by some passing curate on his way to darkest . . . ' He paused, his eyes all mischief. 'Where *do* missionaries go these days?'

Faith didn't know whether to be amused or outraged — realised almost too late that she should be neither. 'I'll ask my father to send you some information, shall I?' she asked, her voice carefully neutral. 'Maybe you could spare a donation.'

He leaned back in his chair. 'I would seriously advise you to reconsider. You're quite unsuited to vicarage life.'

'Do you think so?' His bold statement finally amused Faith, but she resisted the impulse to smile. He didn't need encouraging. Instead she ate a little more trout, sipped her wine. 'I've served a very thorough apprenticeship,' she said at last. 'I know precisely what would be expected of me.'

'Organising the church-cleaning rota, arranging the flowers, taking minutes at the Mothers' Union and the Parish Council meetings?'

She had done them all in an emergency and a lot more besides. 'Well, they all have to be done,' she said quite seriously.

'But not by you.'

Well, in view of Julian's views on the matter, perhaps she'd have to give the Mothers' Union a miss, she agreed silently. But Faith kept that thought to herself. 'You don't know me, Harry.' She turned as she heard footsteps behind her and smiled. 'That was delicious, Mac. Thank you.'

'Aye, well. See what y'make of this.'

'This' was an elegant pastry stuffed with wild mushrooms. She tasted it. 'It's absolutely wonderful, Mac. You should open a restaurant.' Her expansive gesture took in the beautiful manor and the parklands beyond as she turned to Harry. 'You could open a hotel here and Mac would make you a fortune.'

'Well, if I'm ever in need of a fortune, I'll bear that in mind.' Faith caught an undercurrent of awkwardness in the look that passed between Mac and Harry and she realised that nothing on earth would induce Harry to throw open this private paradise to the public.

'I'm afraid I began my career in the small business section of the bank,' she found herself apologising. 'It's hard to break the habit — '

'Banking seems an odd career for a woman,' Harry interrupted smoothly. 'Particularly for a clergyman's daughter.'

'Do you really think so?' She was used to men finding her career a little odd. But although Harry was the most opinionated, pig-headed version of the sex she had ever met she kept the cool, distant smile fixed to her lips. 'The fact is that I discovered a talent for managing money when I took over the parish accounts for my father. It's not all summer fêtes and flower arranging, you know.' Just as well, considering how hopeless she was at bending plant material to her will. 'Perhaps you should tell me what you think would be a more suitable career? Maybe social work would fit the profile?'

He didn't answer, or betray his thoughts by so much as a twitch.

'You think that's flying a little too high?' she probed. 'Of course, I realise I'm only a woman and that a woman's true place is serving the male. A secretary is about as high as her aspirations should reach.'

'That was once a male preserve too,' he reminded her.

'Not since the days of the quill pen,' she snapped, then recovered herself, gave a little shrug. 'Obviously you think I should have followed in my aunt's footsteps and become a nanny.'

Harry, totally unabashed by this cool put-down, merely shrugged. 'You'd certainly have been a lot more useful to me right now.'

Faith, a forkful of food halfway to her mouth, felt like flinging it at him. Instead she smiled sweetly. 'Then, since being useful to you is very low on my list of priorities, I clearly made the right decision.'

Ben's thin, high wail rose from the baby monitor on the table beside her and the creases deepened around Harry's mouth as he smiled back with an equal degree of insincerity.

'I expect he needs changing,' Harry said, somewhat unnecessarily. She had a rough idea of what was expected.

'They do say it's the only opportunity a woman ever has to change a man. I shall take it with enthusiasm.'

'Oh, dear.' He rose to his feet. 'If you view the prospect with enthusiasm then it's obvious that you've never done it before. I'd better come with you to hold your hand.'

Faith had already been provoked into responding far too recklessly to Harry's teasing. It had left her emotionally exposed, wide open to ridicule, and right now all she wanted to do was escape. Ben was offering her a brief respite and she was going to make the best of it.

'Actually, Harry, I have a pretty shrewd idea I'll need both of them if his nappy needs changing, so please don't interrupt your dinner on my account.'

For a moment she thought he was going to argue, then he lifted his wide shoulders in a careless shrug. 'Well, if you think you can manage I'm sure Mac can hold things up in the kitchen.'

Her confidence in her ability to handle one small baby was misplaced. He flung his legs up in the air, yelling with misery as she tried to unfasten the complicated system of poppers that kept his suit on. He wriggled as she wiped him, kicking the talc from her hand so that it scattered everywhere before falling out of reach. Then she couldn't get the nappy tabs to stick because of the talc.

'Oh, great,' she muttered as she

pulled another nappy from the box. But Ben just wanted to play and she couldn't resist him. He was so beautiful. So perfect. Tiny fingers and toes, soft skin, an explosive crop of thick dark hair and eyelashes that any girl would kill for. She dropped a kiss on his tummy before she finally fastened the last of the poppers.

'All done at last? You should have taken the hand I offered.'

She started at the unexpected sound of Harry's voice, wondering just how long he had been standing watching her make a fool of herself. 'No.' She picked him up before turning to face Harry. 'I told you I would manage.'

'And so you have. But it doesn't normally take twenty-five minutes to change one small baby. Even I could do it in less.' He moved towards her, touched her cheek. 'And I'd do it without getting talc all over myself.'

'Really?' She rubbed at her cheek with her wrist, ostensibly to remove the smear of white power but more importantly to obliterate the electric tingle left by the tips of his fingers stirring the downy bloom, stirring feelings that she had long ago put away from her. 'Well, I did warn you,' she said, just a touch shakily. 'Next time he cries you can show me how it's done. But meanwhile I think I'd better go and make a few phone calls to try and find you someone more capable.' She turned quickly away to lay Ben down in his cot.

He took her arm. 'Come and try the pudding Mac has produced in your honour. After your tussle with Ben you deserve it.'

'It wasn't a tussle.' She turned, saw the grin that straightened his mouth and responded helplessly. 'More like a wrestling match. And Ben won on a submission.'

★ ★ ★

Harry looked up from his armchair as she entered the library an hour later.

'Did you manage to find someone?'

She handed him a slip of paper. 'Miss Muriel Kenway will be with you tomorrow afternoon. She usually works as a maternity nurse but she's free for a couple of weeks before her next client is due to deliver.'

'And I'm sure she has impeccable references.'

'I telephoned two of them. Apparently you're very lucky to get her.' She knew that because Miss Kenway had told her so.

'In other words, she's going to cost me a fortune.'

'Is that a problem? You did offer to pay top rates,' she reminded him.

'But that was for you.'

'A waste of money. I have no experience.'

'But you're easy on the eye.'

'I actually had to promise Miss Kenway a little extra to persuade her to come, since she's given up her holiday for you.'

'She really shouldn't have made the

sacrifice.' Then he shrugged. 'I'm sure she'll be Mary Poppins personified.'

'I don't think it would be wise to say that to her.' Miss Kenway hadn't sounded as if she had much of a sense of humour. But then newborn babies probably didn't mind.

Harry picked up her doubts. 'You'd better not have saddled me with some sour old bat,' he warned. 'You promised to stay until you found someone satisfactory. And I'll decide what's satisfactory.'

'Miss Kenway sounded quite charming,' Faith assured him. Not thoroughly charming, just . . . *quite* charming. In fact, just what Mr Harry March deserved. Rather pleased with her verbal games, she offered him a bland smile. 'I just thought that nannies must really hate being called Mary Poppins,' she added, covering her slip. 'I certainly would. Shall I pour you some coffee?'

'Thanks, but I can manage a coffee-pot.' He rose stiffly to his feet, eased his leg then poured two cups, handing one

90

to her. 'Do you play backgammon?' He indicated the board set up on an exquisite games table in the bow of the window.

'Occasionally. My father enjoys a game.' It was actually played as a blood sport at the vicarage, but she wasn't about to tell him that. 'Would you like to play now?'

'Oh, Faith,' he said softly. 'The things you say.'

The blush that darkened her cheeks sealed his fate. Not that he was easy to beat. It had been a while since she'd played and she had rather expected him to indulge her, humour her a little. After all, she was a *woman*. She was mistaken. The speed of the first game took her by surprise and she was swept away. She came back at him in the second, beating him with a double six. After that it was war, and the dice flew and the counters slapped fast and furious around the beautiful antique inlaid board.

It was four games all when Harry

called a halt, glancing at his watch. 'It's late and Ben will have you up at six.'

'I'm on a winning streak,' Faith declared rebelliously, smothering a yawn. 'You just don't want me to beat you.'

Harry grinned. 'You couldn't beat me if you played until Christmas. But I'll let you try. Tomorrow.'

'I won't be here tomorrow.'

★   ★   ★

He was right about the early start. Alice woke her by sitting on her back. 'Ben's awake,' she said, very loudly, very close to her ear. Faith opened her eyes briefly. Then closed them again. Alice tugged at the sleeve of her pyjamas. 'He smells awful. You'll have to change him.' The words didn't make any sense for a moment. Then they did and she groaned. 'That's what Mummy always says too,' Alice said, bouncing back to the floor. 'You'd better hurry, or the whole house will stink.'

Should Alice be allowed to say that? Faith opened her eyes and looked blearily at her watch. It wasn't quite six o'clock. Far too early to worry about what words her small charge used. She'd leave it for the professional to make a ruling.

By half-past she had dealt somewhat queasily, but more successfully than in her previous attempt, with Ben's bottom and the three of them were in the kitchen trying to make up a bottle for his breakfast. It was beginning to be a matter of some urgency, as his cries of hunger threatened to raise the roof.

'Come quickly, Muriel Kenway,' Faith murmured as she finally popped the bottle into Ben's mouth, having carefully followed the instructions on the tin of baby milk, and had them heavily supplemented by well-meaning advice from Alice. Alice began to help herself to cereals, scattering them liberally over the table and floor. Helpless to do more than watch as Ben sucked contentedly from the bottle,

Faith left her to it. She could always clear up afterwards. 'Mind the milk . . . ' Too late. The bottle was knocked over and the table awash.

'It's all right,' Alice said cheerfully as she righted the bottle and poured the remainder over her cereals. 'There's plenty left.'

'Oh, good,' Faith said faintly as, mindless of the mess surrounding her, Alice tucked into her cornflakes.

Being pitched headlong into the day like this was not the way Faith liked to wake up. Her mornings were usually peaceful affairs. Tea. A shower. A little toast and coffee while she contemplated the financial pages.

Ben paused for breath. Should she wind him? She thought she probably should but was unwilling to risk his throwing up over her again. Instead she cradled him in the crook of her arm, nestling him against her breast. He was warm and milky and smiling gummily up at her. Smiling? No, she remembered Aunt Janet saying that babies didn't smile. It was just wind. Oh, well. She put him over her shoulder and began rubbing gently at his back.

She had known it all once. She had stayed with her aunt in the summer holidays and had been her most eager pupil when it had come to babycare. But she had avoided babies since Michael had jilted her. With his desertion she had put all that . . . romance, marriage, two point four children, happy-ever-after . . . behind her. But she didn't want to spend the rest of her life alone. That's why Julian had so appealed to her. The very lack of romance had been a relief, something she could cope with.

Ben's burp dragged her back to the kitchen. At least they had it to themselves. She had half expected the dour Mac to be in possession, even at this early hour, and because of the racket Ben had been making she hadn't dared to waste time getting dressed. But it was still only seven. Plenty of time to clear up and get back to the safety of her room before anyone appeared.

'What the hell . . . ?'

She swung round to discover Harry standing in the kitchen doorway. Far from being tucked up safely in bed, as she had supposed, he had already been out.

His dark hair was wet, dripping onto the white towel hanging about a pair of tanned and powerful shoulders that glistened with moisture. His chest was deep, sprinkled liberally with coarse dark hair that dived across the hard plane of his stomach and disappeared into the sleek blackness of a pair of Speedo briefs. His legs were long, hairy, well muscled, except where a scar, livid and deep, raked his left thigh, puckering the flesh. Something had ripped through it, tearing flesh and bone, and she flinched just for a moment, seeming to feel the pain for herself. His eyes blanked as he took in her shocked expression, and she tried desperately to pull herself together as he turned away to tug on the tracksuit that he was carrying.

She wanted to say something, break

the awful silence. He had gone swimming early because he didn't expect anyone to be around. Because he didn't want to see anyone. Didn't want anyone to see him. But her tongue was like a lump of wood in her mouth. And what could she say? I'm sorry? There didn't seem to be much point in that. Besides, he had already turned his attention to the mess of cereals and milk that puddled the table and had now started to drip steadily onto the floor.

'Just in time for breakfast, I see,' he said curtly.

She dragged her eyes back up to his face and his eyes mocked her imagined weakness, as if he'd expected nothing better. As if he were used to nothing better. What did he expect, for heaven's sake? It had been a shock. But that was all. She had seen worse. He could have lost his leg altogether; in fact she suspected that it had been touch-and-go.

'Your timing is perfect, Harry,' she said, keeping her voice brisk. 'But, as you can see, it's self-service.'

97

4

'Is there any coffee going?' Harry asked abruptly.

'I'm afraid not. I've only one pair of hands and both of them are occupied.'

'I could hardly fail to notice,' he replied, taking in the chaos created by Alice's attempt to make breakfast for herself.

She wasn't sure whether he was angry. It was disconcerting not to be able to tell, impossible to know how to react. Perhaps indifference was safer. But difficult. Harry March wasn't a man anyone could remain indifferent to.

'I think I'd better make some for both of us. Frankly, you look as if you need it.'

Not angry, then, just irritable at having his routine disturbed.

'I'd rather have tea,' she replied. His

disbelief strained her mask of indifference to the limit. 'If it's not too much trouble,' she added, very politely.

He gave her a sharp sideways glance. 'It's a very great deal of trouble and I wouldn't do it if you were a proper nanny,' he said, giving the cereals and dripping milk a wide berth as he went to fill the kettle. His limp seemed more noticeable, or maybe she was just more aware of it now. Impossible not to be.

'If I were a proper nanny, you wouldn't have to. I did warn you.'

'So you did.' Something in his face as he turned back to her suggested that his sense of humour had reasserted itself. 'But if the choice is between a *proper* nanny and you in red silk pyjamas perhaps it isn't such a hardship putting up with you.' Faith, used to living alone, had not stopped to consider the wisdom of coming down to the kitchen with nothing between her and the outside world but a pair of clinging silk pyjamas. 'Julian's choice, were they?' he asked. He was definitely smiling now. It was that particularly irritating smile that made her fingers itch to slap him.

'I don't think that's any of your business,' she said, meaning to put him firmly in his place, but the words came out all wrong. Not crisp and decisive at all. Breathy. Stupid.

Alice had turned to watch this exchange with interest. 'I *like* your 'jamas, Faith. Don't you like them, Uncle Harry?' she demanded.

Faith didn't want to know what Uncle Harry thought of her pyjamas, but he clearly took this as an invitation to give them his most careful consideration. As his gaze trickled slowly over the silk her skin began to prickle and the soft tips of her breasts leapt to attention against the flimsy cloth, responding instinctively to the darkening of his eyes. 'I like them very much, Alice. They are very . . . '

He raised his eyes to hers as Alice impatiently demanded, 'Very what, Uncle Harry?'

Faith's face flamed. She could see

exactly what he thought. She felt it in her response to a look that seemed to quicken her very blood, but she refused to back down, lifting her chin until her eyes clashed head-on with the challenge of the blue.

'Very . . . ' She held her breath as Harry considered his words carefully. 'Very revealing, sweetheart.' She threw down a startled glance but her buttons were all safely fastened. 'They tell me that, beneath the cool, self-possessed façade that Faith has erected against the outside world, there exists a very different girl . . . The kind of girl who drives an Italian sports car, plays backgammon as if her life depends on it . . . ' he paused ' . . . and wears scarlet pyjamas.'

Not understanding her uncle's answer, Alice chose to ignore it. 'Well, I'd like some red 'jamas,' she said. 'They're nice.'

Harry's eyes lingered for the briefest moment upon Faith, clearly enjoying the dark patches of colour that he had brought rushing to her cheeks. 'Yes, sweetheart, they're very nice.' Then he turned to the child. 'Would you like some for your birthday?'

'But you promised me a kitten,' the child declared. 'You haven't forgotten?'

'The kitten isn't for your birthday, Alice. I promised you should have him as soon as he was big enough to leave his mummy.'

Alice's excitement subsided at this unwitting reminder of her own absent mother and instead of eating her cornflakes she began to stir them around her dish, slopping them over the edge, but Faith didn't have the heart to chastise her. By the time Harry had made tea and set coffee to filter she had finished feeding Ben and, determined on a quick getaway, she extended her hand to Alice.

'Come along, Alice. Time to get dressed.'

'Stay and have your tea, Faith. I'll take them both for a walk around the garden. It's a lovely morning.' As he bent over her to lift Ben from her arms she caught the warm, musky scent of his body overlaid with fresh early-morning air. It stirred her senses, rang distant bells in her memory, jarring loose long-buried desires.

She drew back. 'Don't jog him about or he'll be sick,' she warned, keeping her eyes firmly on the baby.

'I'll be careful.'

'And don't go far,' she added, a touch too sharply, as she channelled the dangerous charge of excitement into anxiety for her small charge.

'I'm sure you'll stop me if I do.' His lips said one thing, his eyes, as she foolishly looked up and met them inches from her own, were saying something quite different. It was almost as if he knew how she was feeling, relished the power it gave him. 'Why don't you come with us and make sure?' he invited.

She clutched at the revers of her pyjama jacket in a self-protective gesture. 'I'm not dressed for a stroll in the garden.'

'You're not dressed at all,' he pointed out. 'But I don't mind in the least . . . '

That was it. The teasing had gone quite far enough. Faith stood up, picked up her tea and headed for the door. 'Thanks, but I'll take my tea upstairs and get dressed before I inflict myself upon the day. Alice, if you're not going to eat that, please leave it alone . . . ' She caught herself. She was beginning to sound just like her aunt. 'Are you sure you don't mind looking after them for a few minutes?' she asked Harry.

'You can cook me some breakfast as a reward for my good deed,' he replied. It was as if he was determined to provoke her, got some kind of buzz from seeing her cheeks heat up. But she refused to play.

'With pleasure, but I hope you don't expect Miss Kenway to cook for you.'

'No. But then I don't expect Miss Kenway to leave me holding the baby either. Don't be long.'

She wasn't long. The fastest shower

in history was followed by the equally speedy donning of a pair of jeans and the spare T-shirt she had brought with her. She tied her hair back, fastened an apron about her waist and by the time Harry reappeared the kitchen was clean and tidy and the aroma of coffee was wafting pleasantly about the room.

'That's some transformation.'

'It was just a few cornflakes and a drop of milk.'

'Who said I was talking about the kitchen?' He held out Ben and, when she took him, poured himself some coffee. 'He usually has a bit of a nap, then a bath, then another bottle and something disgusting from a jar. I think.'

'It would help if you could be a little more positive, since I haven't got a clue.'

'You're doing just fine.'

'If you're trying to tempt me to stay with compliments, Harry, I'm afraid it won't work. Come along, Alice, time to get washed and dressed.' She glanced over her shoulder. 'You can wait a few

minutes for your breakfast, can't you?'
Then she frowned. 'Where's Mac? Has
he gone early-morning fishing?'

'I've no idea.'

'Oh. It's just . . . I thought that he
did the cooking.'

'He does, occasionally, but we don't
live together, Faith.'

'I didn't mean . . . ' Just in time she
realised he was teasing her. Another
word and she'd have been blushing
again. 'You . . . um . . . '

'Just live in the same house?' he
finished for her, with a gentleness that
did not deceive her for a moment. 'Is
that what you meant?'

'Of course that's what I meant.'

'If that's what you thought, Faith,
I'm afraid I have to disillusion you. Mac
has his own place down by the river.'

'Oh,' she said. 'Oh.' And then she did
blush. Although why spending the night
alone in a house with Harry March was
worse than spending the night alone
with two men, she refused to contemplate. But he knew. And, as she fled, a

rich, tormenting peal of laughter followed her up the stairs.

It took her longer than she'd thought possible to sort out the children, and when she returned to the kitchen, leaving Alice determined to tie her own shoelaces if it took all morning, Harry had showered and was wearing a dark suit, a burgundy and white striped shirt and a silk tie, all stamped with the kind of understated elegance that made heads turn without quite knowing why . . . Not the kind of clothes to sit around in at home.

'I'm sorry I was so long,' she said, turning away to pour a cup of coffee she didn't want to cover a ridiculous, unexpected confusion at the intimacy of sharing an early-morning kitchen with him. 'What would you like for breakfast?'

'I'll leave it. If I don't go now I'll be late for an appointment.'

'You really shouldn't miss break-fast — '

'It's the most important meal of the

day. The law according to Janet,' he finished for her, and she looked up to find him regarding her wryly.

'It's true, nevertheless. You should have something . . . ' Her voice faded as she realised just how close he was, that the kitchen table at her back prevented a strategic retreat.

'What do you suggest?'

'A slice of t-toast?' she offered, standing her ground, although his jacket brushed tantalisingly against her arm, raising goose-flesh. 'Or something . . . '

'Or something.' His eyes finally creased in a smile in which all the mockery was directed at himself. 'What a pity you are so determined on leaving, Faith. You offer apparently endless opportunities for entertainment, but regrettably I have an appointment I cannot miss. It's with my bank manager so I know you'll understand how important it is not to be late.'

She was trembling. It should have been with rage but she was honest enough to admit, at least to herself, that it wasn't anything so simple.

Harry, however, was apparently unaffected by the racketing of adrenalin that was coursing through her bloodstream. 'What time did you say this Kenway woman will be arriving?' he asked, as if nothing had happened.

Happened? Nothing *had* happened. He had simply been teasing her. He probably flirted with every woman he met, young and old, pretty and plain. It made them into his slaves. But not her. *Not her.* She'd been Michael's slave, following him about like a doting puppy since she had been old enough to escape her mother's watchful eye, always there, driving him mad when he'd been a teenager, still there when he'd come home from university, grown out of her braces and puppy-fat and ready to become a woman. 'Early afternoon,' she said, with commendable assurance.

He nodded. 'Please don't leave until I get back, Faith. I don't want the children left with a total stranger. No matter how good her references are.'

The assurance fled. 'Won't Mac be around?' He glanced up at the slightly desperate edge to her voice.

'Why should he be?'

'He seemed to be helping out . . . '

'He has a life of his own, Faith, and you promised to stay.'

'Couldn't you put off your appointment? I was hoping to leave this morning.'

'Before you've seen your replacement safely installed? Would you leave your children in the care of a stranger on the word of someone you'd never met?'

She shook her head, ashamed that her own desperation to leave had affected her judgement so badly. 'No, of course not. I'm sorry.' He must have seen something of her feelings in her face, because he laid his hand reassuringly on her shoulder.

'Don't worry, Faith, I'm sure you'll cope brilliantly.' Then he spoilt it by adding, 'Being *renowned* for your level-headedness.'

Her wobbly knees mocked her. *Level-headed?* Had she actually said that? Very well. What would the sensible, the very level-headed Faith do right now? Cover all possibilities, of course. 'Will you please leave a telephone number where I can contact you? In case of an emergency.'

'The numbers of the car phone and the bank are programmed into the telephone.' He nodded to the instrument fixed to the kitchen wall. 'I'm having lunch at Simpson's and then I'm calling in at the hospital to see Janet. I promised you that I would take her roses from the garden, if you remember.'

'You said you were going to send them . . . ' She blurted the words out without thinking and she expected his mockery, but he didn't smile.

Instead he asked, 'Would you really rather I stayed here?' She caught at her lip as for one dizzy moment she thought she was going to blurt out, Yes . . . please.

'No,' she said quickly. Before she could change her mind. And she laughed the very idea to scorn. 'No, of course not. I'll be fine. Please give Janet my love.' She pushed back a stray strand of hair that had sprung loose from her clip. 'Tell her I'll be in to see her tomorrow.'

'I'll give her your love. The rest of your message will only make her fret.' He never missed a trick to make her feel bad about Janet, she thought, but as long as she remembered that it wasn't Janet's welfare that prompted his concern but a determination to get his own way she would be all right. 'I should be back by around four. And you won't be quite on your own. Mrs Williams comes up from the village every morning with a couple of ladies who battle to keep the dust under control. She'll make lunch and offer you motherly advice if you need it.'

'Wouldn't it be easier if she just took over?'

'Poor Faith. So desperate to get away.' He stretched out long fingers and briefly touched her cheek. 'I'll see you later.'

Long after the soft murmur of his engine had faded down the lane, the spot where his fingers had touched her cheek still burned. It was as if he had imprinted her with his mark. Claimed her. But for what?

She shook her head. 'Pull yourself together, Faith Bridges,' she told herself sternly. After all, no young woman *renowned* for her level-headedness would throw her cap over the windmill for a practised charmer with a track record for breaking hearts. Would she? Love was such a fleeting thing, as both she and Clementine Norwood knew to their cost. Besides, she meant what she'd said. She was spoken for. Julian Fellowes was a man whose ideals and beliefs she had grown to respect. Respect and share. They provided a solid foundation for their relationship. That was why she was planning to marry him three weeks on Saturday.

Yet she still felt the brand of Harry's fingers on her cheek. 'Oh, this is ridiculous,' she said aloud, and rubbed at the spot with the heel of her hand. Then she turned and saw Alice looking at her doubtfully from the doorway, her shoelaces tied in neat bows. After so much effort it seemed unkind to point out that her trainers were on the wrong feet. She'd think of a reason to part the child from her shoes, but right now she wasn't feeling that bright. 'Come on, Alice,' she said, taking her own good advice to heart. 'I'm going to have a boiled egg. And since you didn't eat more than a mouthful of cornflakes I think you should have one too.'

'A dippy egg? With soldiers?'

The words brought her aunt vividly to mind and she glanced at her watch. She would already be in the theatre and she took a moment to offer a silent prayer for her before turning back to Alice. 'Toast soldiers?' she asked.

★   ★   ★

After that the morning sped by. Bathing Ben took half the time. She knew how it should be done in theory. Her aunt had shown her with her own baby-sized doll when she had been nine years old.

But dolls didn't wiggle or kick or soak you right through to the skin. She stripped off her T-shirt and donned her silk shirt from the night before. It was all she had left to wear.

Then Mrs Williams, whose excuse for not taking charge of Ben and Alice was an extensive family of her own, advised a walk before lunch. 'Then they'll both sleep this afternoon,' she said, with the confidence of years of experience.

Lunch for Ben was something gloopy from a jar, most of which splattered her expensive silk shirt, but she had nothing to change into and was too exhausted to care very much.

At least there was no time to think about Harry March until she had put the two children down for an afternoon nap, when she collapsed in the kitchen chair with a cup of tea, trying to resist the very pleasant idea of having one herself. The urgent summons of the telephone saved her from the shaming temptation.

'Wickham Hall,' she answered.

'Miss Bridges? It's Muriel Kenway.'

Faith glanced at her watch. She had been expecting the woman to arrive at any moment. 'Miss Kenway? Are you lost?'

'Lost? Oh, no.' She cleared her throat. 'The fact is . . . well, I told you my client wasn't due to deliver for another two weeks but . . . ' She hesitated.

'But what, Miss Kenway?'

'Well, babies are no respecters of timetables.'

'It's arrived early? Are they both all right?' Faith enquired.

'Both? Um, yes . . . fortunately her husband caught me just as I was leaving,' she rushed on. 'You do understand?' Muriel Kenway had struck her as the kind of woman not to be fazed by anything. Now she sounded so anxious that Faith felt she had to reassure her.

'It can't be helped. Please don't worry; I'll manage here until I can make some other arrangements.'

'Yes. Of course you will. Goodbye.'

Faith stared at the phone for a moment, then hung up. 'I don't seem to have any choice.' She caught sight of her bespattered shirt and groaned. She'd have to tackle the secrets of the washing machine. But not before she spent a frantic half-hour leaving messages with everyone she could think of who might be able to help.

* * *

'How was Aunt Janet?' Harry had taken Nanny Kenway's defection with remarkable equanimity. But then he had no reason to be in the least bit concerned. He already had her assurance that she would stay until she could find someone to take her place. Now, comfortably settled in an ancient armchair that sagged in front of the kitchen range, he stopped kneading the muscles in his thigh and propped his leg upon the fender, stretching his other leg across a yard of quarry-tiled floor, and took the tea she had made for him.

'Still dozy from the anaesthetic. But everything went well. I met your father at the hospital, by the way. Nice man. He seemed surprised you were down here.' Harry glanced up at her, the deep creases in his cheeks betraying some hidden source of entertainment. 'And more than a little amused.'

Laughing his clerical-grey socks off at the thought probably. 'Really?' Faith said chillingly, not in the least bit pleased to think of the two men discussing her. 'What did he say?'

'Oh, nothing.' His slow smile suggested otherwise. 'Except . . . '

'What?'

'Not to expect too much since you were hopelessly undomesticated and . . . '

She wasn't about to argue with that. 'And what?' she demanded.

'He warned me never to play backgammon with you, since you can't bear to lose.'

'Neither can he. And I haven't lost,'

she reminded him, with considerable satisfaction.

'Not yet. But now you're staying I intend to change all that.'

'In your dreams, Harry,' she murmured as the baby alarm warned her that Ben was awake. 'Feeding time at the zoo,' she said as she headed for the kitchen door.

'You do rather look as if you've been serving at the chimps' tea-party,' he agreed.

'I've run out of clean clothes,' she replied pointedly.

'And it didn't occur to you to use the washing machine?'

'I didn't expect to be staying this long.'

He grinned. 'Well, I'll look you out a clean T-shirt to be going along with, but I can see what your father meant about a disinclination for domesticity.'

'Oh, can you? Then if you're wise you'll send out for a pizza,' she retaliated as she retreated through the kitchen door.

But Harry March was way ahead of her, and when she returned to the kitchen to give Ben his supper she found the promised T-shirt together with a note. 'I've taken Alice down to the river for a picnic. Put Ben in his buggy and join us.'

An order or an invitation? He clearly didn't expect her to say no, but then, who had ever said no to Harry March? Then she shook her head at her own foolishness. Level-headed, remember? Sensible. Quite capable of handling a sultry evening on the riverbank with a man, no matter how irresistible. And besides, Alice and Ben made perfect chaperons. Not that she would need them.

She fed Ben and, having finally begun to get the hang of babies, within half an hour she was dressed in a baggy white T-shirt which fitted where it touched and reached almost to her knees and wheeling the bright little buggy towards the river. As she rounded a bend in the path she was driven to admit to herself that Harry March had style.

A thick white cloth was spread upon the grass and on it reposed the contents of a wicker hamper supplied by a London store famous for such treats. The plates had been brought from the house and were of fine bone china, the wineglasses were old, hand-blown crystal and the cutlery fashioned by some master silversmith to grace a Georgian table.

He glanced up as he heard her approach. 'As you can see, I took your advice and arranged a take-away.'

'It wasn't quite what I had in mind,' she murmured, parking the buggy beneath a willow tree and, after spreading a net across it to keep insects from the infant, leaving him to enjoy the shadowy movement of the leaves above him. 'Where I come from 'take-away' suggests a spur-of-the-moment choice between a pizza and a curry.'

'They wouldn't have travelled well, so I picked this up on my way home instead.'

'Clearly you took my father's warning seriously to heart.'

'Not really. I just thought you might be feeling in need of a little pampering. Looking after children is pretty exhausting, even when you're used to it.'

'That's very thoughtful of you,' she said primly, firmly ignoring her body's over-excited response to the idea of being pampered by Harry, reminding herself that Julian was eagerly awaiting that pleasure. At least, she was sure he was. He hadn't actually written and said so. But then his letters were so full of his work . . . She gave herself a gentle mental shaking and surveyed the picnic. Then her brows drew together with a tiny frown.

'What's wrong?'

'Nothing,' she said slowly. 'I really do appreciate the trouble you've gone to. But haven't you forgotten something?'

'Have I?' His glance roved swiftly over the cloth. 'Oh, you mean the wine. Don't worry — it's keeping cool in the river.'

She refused to show her exasperation. 'I don't mean the wine, Harry, I mean me.'

'But you're here.'

'That's my point. I'm not supposed to be here. I'm supposed to be on my way back to London. Remember?'

'And you don't think Nanny Kenway would have been tempted by my feast?'

'I'm sure you could tempt the stars, Harry.'

'Are you? Well, that's a promising start.'

'No, it isn't, and I'm sure that Nanny Kenway would not have been quite such a pushover. By now she would certainly have had the children tucked up in bed and be doing something thoroughly worthy like ironing,' she replied, more interested in Harry's ploy of avoiding her question by asking one of his own than pandering to his ego.

'You'd be surprised how vulnerable the Muriel Kenways of this world are to flattery. Crack the shell and the yolk is all soft and dippy.'

'Like Aunt Janet?' she murmured.

'Like Janet,' he agreed. 'Alice likes these little pieces of chicken,' he continued, holding out a plate to his niece. 'Why don't you find something you like while I open the wine?'

Instinct warned her that he was trying to distract her. But why? 'Did you buy off Muriel Kenway?' she demanded as suspicion suddenly jagged her. 'Just to keep me here?' Even as she said it she realised how ridiculous she must sound. How neurotic. Why on earth would he go to such lengths? All he wanted was a temporary nanny, for heaven's sake. 'I'm sorry,' she said quickly, looking away from eyes that had narrowed in a fierce question. A question to which there were no answers. 'I didn't mean that. It's just that everything seems to be conspiring to keep me here when I — '

'When you have so much to do somewhere else,' he finished for her thoughtfully. 'What have you got to do, Faith? What is it that simply won't wait a week or two?'

'I . . . ' Still she hesitated, although why she was so unwilling to tell him she didn't know. Or, maybe, just wouldn't admit.

'Is it so very bad?' Harry asked gently.

'Bad?' She stared at the lobster tail she had peeled, as if uncertain what it was or where it had come from.

'Whatever it is you have to do, Faith, you don't seem to be very happy about it.'

'Happy?' The word had such a ramshackle quality. People put such faith in the notion that they should be happy that they were bound to be hurt. When she had received Julian's letter suggesting they should get married it had been a surprise. Of course it had. They had been writing to one another for three years but they had never actually met. Yet they agreed on everything. They had so much in common. It had seemed so . . . sensible, so logical. Right now she couldn't quite think why, but it would seem that way again, she knew it. Just as soon as she could get away from the unsettling Harry March. 'Of course I'm happy!' she declared.

The broad space between his brows creased in a frown. 'Then why don't you try smiling?' For a moment their eyes clashed, then he shrugged. 'I do understand that your business is infinitely more important than mine, and, I promise, I do appreciate you staying on. Perhaps there is some way I can prove it to you. Is there anything I can do to help?'

'Like what?' She couldn't meet his eyes. 'I'm sorry. I didn't mean to snap, it's just . . . '

'Just?' he prompted.

'If you must know, Harry, I'm getting married in three weeks and I haven't even bought the dress yet . . . '

5

A sudden quiet greeted this announcement, leaving her voice seemingly echoing off the water, forlornly repeating the word . . . 'married' . . . 'married' . . . 'married' . . . and Harry's long fingers stilled in the act of peeling the foil from the champagne cork.

'Why?' His voice was quiet but insistent.

She looked up then, surprised by something in his voice. Concern? Could it be concern? 'Why haven't I bought the dress yet?'

'No, Faith. Why are you getting married?'

She stiffened. 'I'm not preg — ' She broke off, looking anxiously at Alice, who had wandered over to a pair of ducks and was happily feeding them a roll. 'Alice come back, darling.'

'You can't avoid my question that easily, Faith.'

'I told you, I'm not — '

'Of course you're not. Level-headed women don't get pregnant unless they want to, although love makes fools of us all.'

'I'm not in love!' His brows rose and she flushed. 'I'm sorry,' she muttered, feeling stupid. How on earth could he be expected to understand?

'Sorry that you're getting married, or sorry that you're not — ?'

'Will you stop that?' He shrugged and she made an effort to regain her poise. 'I have to return to London, Harry. You must see that.'

'Why? You could arrange everything from here. There's the telephone, the fax, the Internet.' He paused. 'There's even a very good bridal shop in Melchester.' It was her turn to raise her eyebrows. 'So I'm told.'

'By Clementine Norwood?' Reminding him of the girl he had so callously jilted seemed to offer her a safety net. Reminding herself why she didn't trust to love.

There was a momentary tightening of the muscles about his jaw but nothing else to suggest she had disturbed him. 'Clemmie, wear a ready-made dress? I'd like to see the day.' His fingers grasped the cork and he twisted the champagne bottle sharply. The cork came away with a restrained burp and the wine foamed into two glasses. 'Elizabeth went there to buy her gown. She never fails to remind me of that fact when she comes to stay.'

'Your matchmaking sister?'

'The very same.' He offered a smile and the tension evaporated in its warmth.

'Not very subtle, is she?'

'Not in the least.' His mouth straightened in a grin and she found herself responding quite helplessly. Irresistible. He didn't need any help from his sister to find a wife, she decided. But it was seven years since he had abandoned Clementine, the same seven years since Michael had abandoned her. So why . . . ? She caught herself. It was absolutely none of her business. 'Well? What do you say?' he prompted.

She wavered. A lot of the things she had to do could be dealt with long distance, but it wasn't quite that simple. 'I don't think I could manage it all and look after the children as well. And I'm rather short of clothes.'

'You're welcome to help yourself to mine.'

She tugged at the oversized T-shirt. 'Oh, gee, thanks.'

'Don't you like it? Women look so vulnerable in men's clothes.' His eyes swept her figure. 'Sexy, too — '

'And the children?' she interrupted, determined to put an end to this dangerous conversation.

He shrugged. 'You underestimate yourself, Faith. But I'm sure that if you insist on marrying your missionary we could arrange things between us — '

'He's not *my* missionary! He's not a missionary at all!' It was better when he made her angry. Easier. 'He's a scientist.'

'A scientist?' he repeated thoughtfully, lifting a glass to offer it to her. 'A scientist who is difficult to contact? Where is he, Faith? Paddling down the Amazon in a canoe?'

'Not quite.' Her sense of humour almost returned at this stab in the dark that was so wide of the mark.

'His canoe has a motor?'

'You're not even close. Wrong continent altogether. He's in the Antarctic,' she said.

'*The Antarctic?*' She had finally managed to surprise him, and she took the champagne with barely a tremor despite the brief touch of his fingers against hers. 'And are you planning to join him in his research after the wedding? Or will you wait patiently at home for his occasional visit? I can't believe that penguins have much use for bankers.'

'Penguins? Don't be ridiculous.'

'*I'm* being ridiculous? You're the one planning to live at the South Pole.' He spun the stem of the champagne flute

131

in his hand. 'With a man you're not in love with.' She kept her mouth firmly shut. She had already said far too much. But he wasn't going to let her get away without some explanation. 'Is that the reason for the rush? Does he have to get back to his experiments?'

Relief that he hadn't asked the obvious question loosened her tongue. 'Is it so impossible to imagine that Julian might just be anxious to marry me as quickly as possible?'

'Far from impossible. I can't imagine how he's managed to keep himself away. But what about you?'

'Me too,' she said quickly. Too quickly, perhaps.

'Are you sure? Most women about to get married can't stop talking about it. You seem markedly reluctant to even mention the fact.'

'The only thing I'm markedly reluctant to do, Harry, is to provide you with a source of amusement.'

'I can assure you that I don't find the prospect of your imminent marriage in the least bit funny.' He said it as if he meant it, although what possible interest it was to him she couldn't think.

'You keep making jokes about Julian,' she reminded him.

'And Julian, it seems, is no joking matter.'

She gave him a hard look, but he seemed perfectly genuine. 'No, he isn't. So you must understand why I'm anxious to get back to London. I have to organise everything and there's so much to do. The reception, for instance. I was supposed to be seeing the caterers yesterday to discuss the buffet but I had to cancel the meeting.'

'To come rushing to my rescue?'

She gave him a chilling look. 'And then there are the invitations. The proofs have to be checked and then they'll have to be written and sent. Dad's organising the church, of course, but I can't leave the flowers and the cake to him . . . ' Harry had accused her of being unwilling to talk about her wedding; suddenly she seemed unable to stop.

'Haven't you forgotten the most important thing?' She refused to ask what he meant. 'Your wedding dress?'

She seized on this excuse with gratitude. 'I haven't even begun to look at wedding dresses, so you see how it is . . .'

Alice, having finished her roll, had returned to plunder the picnic for more treats for the ducks. Mention of a wedding, however, drove them from her mind. 'Can I be your bridesmaid, Faith? My friend Charlotte was a bridesmaid.'

'I'm sure that Faith knows a lot of little girls who want to be her bridesmaid,' Harry intervened.

'I'm just having two of my own friends, Alice. Grownup bridesmaids.' She glanced at Harry. 'I was meeting them as well, but I've had to leave them to organise their own dresses.'

'Why don't you leave everything to them?' he suggested.

'It's *my* wedding.'

Alice tugged at her sleeve. 'Well, could I be a flower girl, then? My friend Charlotte was a flower girl when her — '

'Alice,' Harry said firmly, 'you have to wait to be asked.'

Alice turned to Faith, her eyes very big, very blue, just like her Uncle Harry's, and waited to be asked. 'I could bring my own flowers,' she prompted hopefully. 'Uncle Harry would let me pick some from his garden.'

Faith floundered, melted, found herself saying, 'Well, perhaps just one flower girl . . . if your mummy doesn't mind . . . ' She couldn't believe that she was doing this.

'Oh, Elizabeth won't mind,' Harry said confidently. 'She'll just be grateful that Alice will at last be able to get one up on the ghastly Char — ' Faith glared and he turned 'Charlotte' into a cough. 'If she isn't home by then I'll bring Alice myself. I'd be interested to meet your missionary.'

'He's not — ' She stopped. There was no point in repeating herself endlessly. He was only doing it to annoy her. His smile, all strong white even teeth, proved it.

'Can we buy my dress tomorrow?' Alice asked.

'Your dress?' Faith felt the ground being swept relentlessly from beneath her feet. Another complication. As if there weren't enough already.

'Flower girls have to have special dresses,' Alice informed her importantly. 'My friend Charlotte had a pink one. With lots of frills. And ribbons. And she had pink satin shoes and flowers in her hair — '

'Pink ones?' Harry intervened somewhat drily and Alice nodded happily. 'How ever did I guess?' Faith bit her lower lip to prevent herself emitting a slightly hysterical laugh. Clearly Alice was taking the whole thing very seriously. 'We'll go into Melchester tomorrow, sweetheart, and choose one,' he continued. 'If Faith doesn't mind?' The look he turned on her was darkly amused, like the devil in a good mood, she thought as the desire to laugh rapidly deserted her. Only the hysteria remained. 'It will give you a chance to look at wedding dresses. Maybe you could find one with lots of frills and ribbons to suit you as well . . . '

'Are you mad?' Faith was finally driven to demand. 'Bridal shops don't expect the bride to bring along a parcel of *children* to the fitting. *They* usually come later.'

'Usually,' he agreed. She felt the treacherous colour rise to her cheeks, but he was refilling her glass and didn't seem to notice. 'We'll have to take Alice, anyway,' he pointed out. 'And Ben will sleep through most of it if we time it right. We'd better leave straight after breakfast. And don't worry about the rest of your organising. If only you'd explained yesterday instead of being so ridiculously coy. Heavens, anyone would think you weren't eager — '

'Of course I'm eager!' Last week she had been bubbling with plans, had had her lists all drawn up, hadn't been able to wait to get started on the arrangements. Then Harry March, with his blue eyes and scar-riven face, had sent Janet a frantic SOS and now her life was getting more complicated by the minute. 'Do you think I'd get engaged on some . . . some whim?' she demanded.

He regarded her thoughtfully. 'People get engaged for all sorts of reasons — '

'Do they?' She interrupted him before he could ask her reason for marrying Julian. 'So why did you get engaged to Miss Clementine Norwood when you had no intention of marrying her? Tell me that.' Then, as she realised what she had said, her hand flew to her mouth as if to stop the words. But it was too late.

Harry's mouth had tightened almost imperceptibly, his blue eyes taking on a steely tone in the shadows beneath the willow, and as he reached for her hand and pulled it away from her mouth, as if to see for himself the lips that had uttered such shocking words, her heart began to pound with an intensity that almost choked her.

Alice had wandered off to pick daisies so that she could practise her role as flower girl. Ben was sleeping. The only sound was that of the world turning to the accompaniment of the river and the sleepy quacking of the ducks settling down for the night.

'Well?' Harry asked, very quietly. 'Have you finally lost your tongue?'

'Not lost it,' Faith murmured, desperate to look away but unable to escape eyes like hot sapphires. 'But my foot seems to be stuck in my mouth. Right up to the ankle.'

'This will help,' he said with unexpected sympathy, refilling her glass and putting it in her hand before releasing her. Then, his face close to hers, he touched his own glass to hers. 'To promises, Faith.'

'Promises?' she asked uncertainly.

'Promises,' he affirmed. 'And, despite everything that Janet taught us, the hard-won knowledge that not all of them should be kept.'

Faith froze, the glass halfway to her lips. 'Not — ?'

'The trick is knowing which ones.'

She scrambled to her feet, furious with herself for being drawn into the warm, tempting circle that he was closing about her. But what else should she expect? The man was a past master at breaking promises. 'I think it's time Alice was in the bath,' she said abruptly, and didn't wait for his reply but called the child to her as she released the brake on the buggy and, ignoring the fact that her legs were shaking uncontrollably, wheeled it away.

★　★　★

'Faith? I was just coming to look for you.'

She paused a few steps above him on the stairs, feeling foolish after her abrupt departure from the picnic, knowing that she had overreacted to his teasing. 'I've been putting the children to bed,' she said. And taking as long about it as she could.

'Someone left a message on the answering machine for you. You'd better hear it for yourself.' He didn't wait for her agreement, but simply turned and led the way to the room beneath the stairs.

'Faith? It's Debbie. I've found you a nanny. She used to work for my sister. Will you ring me straight back?'

Harry switched off the machine. 'I assume you know her number, since she didn't leave it.'

'Or you'd have called back and told her that you were all fixed up?'

Harry's brows lifted in innocent query. 'Now why on earth would I do that?'

'I can't think, except that you seem to be deriving considerable amusement from my enforced stay.'

'Enforced?' He refused to respond to her tetchiness, but his glance flickered briefly over her in a manner calculated to irritate. 'I don't see any chains.'

Perhaps 'enforced' was a little harsh, she admitted privately to herself. She could walk out any time she chose. Except that she had promised Janet she would stay and help and he was using that promise to save himself the bother of finding someone else to look after his sister's children. It would just serve him right if she decided that this was a promise she didn't need to keep, she thought crossly. Except that she didn't find it as easy to break inconvenient promises as he did. 'You know perfectly well what I mean,' she said.

'Perhaps I do,' he admitted. 'Maybe it's just something about your desperation to get away that challenges me. And I never could resist a challenge. To my cost.' His lips were smiling — just — but disconcertingly the joke didn't seem to be quite reaching his eyes, and Faith wondered just what challenge had left him scarred and limping. 'But relief, apparently, is at hand. Who was that?'

'Debbie and I went to school

together. In fact,' she went on with considerable relish, 'she's going to be one of my bridesmaids.' Now why had she said that? Simply to make a point? What point, for heaven's sake? That in three weeks come Saturday she was going to marry Julian Fellowes in her father's church? As if Harry March would care one way or the other. 'I'd better ring her back.'

'Help yourself,' he invited, with an expansive gesture at the steel-grey bulk of his communications network. Were these the electronics he 'played around with', she wondered? If so, it seemed to be rather more than a game.

Faith waited for him to leave, but he propped himself against the desk, deciding, correctly, that this would annoy her most. Well, it didn't matter one way or another, she thought, punching the number into the keypad. She didn't care whether he listened or not, just as long as it got her out of here.

Debbie bubbled with enthusiasm.

143

'Sarah's a real gem. My niece adored her, but when Emily started school at Easter Sarah decided to work as a temporary nanny rather than take another long-term post. I think she found it difficult letting go of her after so long. It must be difficult, don't you think?'

'Very difficult,' said Faith. Her aunt had never been able to forget the children she had worked with. She still followed their lives in the society magazines and newspapers — she glanced at Harry — still rushed to their aid at the first hint of trouble. 'If you'll give me her number, I'll call her straight away.' She jotted down the details on a notepad by the phone and then exchanged a few words about bridesmaids' dresses, with Debbie describing the dresses that she and Gemma had provisionally chosen. 'They sound lovely, Debbie; I'll leave it to you.'

'The wedding's still on, then? You've not got . . . er . . . cold feet?'

'That's not funny!'

'Hey, girl! What's happened to your

sense of humour?'

Faith did not reply.

'I'll . . . um . . . pick the dresses up tomorrow, then, shall I? If you're sure about the colour?'

'The green sounds lovely,' Faith said firmly, wondering why no one was taking her determination to marry Julian in the least bit seriously. 'I'll be glad to have something I can cross off my list.'

'Your bridesmaids are wearing green?' Harry asked when she replaced the receiver. 'Isn't that supposed to be unlucky at a wedding?'

'Is it?' She dialled again, glad of something to do with her hands that prevented her from throttling Harry. Or at least slapping that irritating expression from his face. The line was engaged. 'Since I'm not superstitious I won't lose any sleep over it. Anyway, they're hardly green,' she said, turning to him with the kind of look that had been known to turn flirtatious bank clerks to jelly. 'It's just a very fine green stripe on ivory.'

'I'm sure Janet wouldn't approve.' Oh, he was right about that. But it had nothing to do with the colour of bridesmaids' dresses. Janet disapproved of everything about her wedding but she wasn't going to hand Mr Harry March a gift of such information — always assuming that her aunt hadn't already given him chapter and verse.

'It's my wedding,' she pointed out, and he lifted his shoulders in an apparently careless shrug.

'It actually takes two, Faith, but if you're prepared to take the risk then I suppose it's up to you.'

Harry and her aunt would make a great double act she thought a little sourly as he straightened. But Janet Bridges had a right to be concerned about her only niece. What possible interest was it to this man?

'Well, I'll leave you to get on with it. I'm sure you're quite capable of handling the details.'

'There's only one problem. Debbie says Sarah can't get here until late tomorrow evening.'

His lips curled tauntingly. 'That's your problem, Faith, not mine, but at least it means we'll have plenty of time for our shopping trip tomorrow.'

'Oh, but — '

'Alice is so looking forward to it. Unless, of course, you've changed your mind about her being your flower girl? Now that you've organised your escape route?'

Escape route? Did she seem that desperate to get away? Well, that wouldn't do, she thought, so she made herself smile. 'I wasn't aware that I was a prisoner, Harry,' she said, with the smallest laugh.

'You were the one who suggested it, not me.' And he was right. The wretched man was right. She felt like screaming. 'If you want to leave right now . . . ' He offered her the door, and for one crazy moment she came close to bolting through it.

'Don't be silly, Harry,' she said, as calmly as she could. 'I'll stay until

Sarah arrives. And of course I haven't changed my mind about Alice being a flower girl. I promised.'

'And a promise is a promise?' That cynical toast beneath the willow tree stirred the air between them. 'It's an admirable sentiment. I wonder just how far you'd be prepared to take it?'

'I wouldn't ever make a promise I wasn't prepared to keep,' she said quietly. Unlike Michael. Unlike Harry.

'But you rather had your hand forced by Alice. And by Janet. What about Julian? Did he blackmail you too?'

'I'm not quite as weak-willed as you appear to think.'

'Not weak-willed. Just a little too kind for your own good, Faith.' The smile was back in place, although whether that was something to congratulate herself on she couldn't be quite sure.

'And that's a weakness you are very happy to take advantage of,' she snapped.

'Did I say it was a weakness?' She didn't answer. 'But Alice will need a dress . . . Of course you could leave *her* to choose something appropriate. Do you think pink frills will go with the elegant green and ivory?' he enquired gravely.

The problem with Harry, Faith decided as she capitulated with a laugh, was that no matter how infuriating he was you just couldn't stay mad at him for long. 'You should take up blackmail full-time, Harry. You're very good at it. I'll come and choose it with her.'

'And what about your dress?' he continued tormentingly. 'Will you be looking for something bedecked with frills and ribbons for your big day?'

'Frills . . . ?' Eighteen and head over heels in love had been a time for frills. 'I'm allergic to frills, Harry. In fact I'd rather be married in a black plastic sack.'

'Now that would be entertaining.' His thoughtful look rang alarm bells, and to distract him she changed tack.

'I wonder if I could take you up on your offer to ring the printer in the morning and ask him to fax through the proofs of the invitations?' she asked. 'I really can't afford to lose another day. I was hoping to have them written and in the post by the beginning of next week.'

'Then I hope for your sake it isn't going to be a big wedding.'

'Big enough.' Julian hadn't much of a family and she would have been happy enough to limit the guests to close friends, but there were so many parishioners who had become an extended family after her mother died. Not one of them could be missed off the list.

'What about the caterers? Surely they'll fax their menus here too if we ask them? It seems a pity to have all this high-tech equipment and not use it, don't you think?'

Faith looked around her. 'It's a pretty fancy toy,' she agreed.

'Toy?'

'Isn't this another of your toys? You did say you 'play around' with electronics.'

'Did I?' His smile was disconcerting. 'Well, from now on my *toy* is entirely at your disposal. Look out those numbers and I'll deal with it after you've phoned this new female.'

Despite his faintly mocking tone, he seemed perfectly willing to help, and because it would make everything a whole lot easier she agreed. After phoning Sarah and giving her directions to Wickham Ash, she gave him the information he had asked for and went off to check on the children.

They were both sleeping peacefully, and as she walked from bed to cot, adjusting the covers, smoothing back a tiny lock of hair, Faith felt a tug of longing . . . She began to understand her aunt's feelings towards her charges. Even after such a short time it would be hard to say goodbye.

'All sleeping?' Harry whispered, coming up behind, putting his hand on her shoulder as he leaned over the cot. His touch was so natural, so warm and it was such a long time since she had been touched by anyone . . .

'It's been a long day for all of us,' she

said, a little hoarsely.

'Don't give up on it yet. Come and have a drink and give me a chance to get my own back at backgammon.'

'You don't stand a chance,' she said automatically as she turned. For a moment he remained blocking her way, his hand still resting lightly on her shoulder.

'No?' The word fell softly into the peaceful room, scarcely more than a whisper, and yet it was a challenge, a dare that Faith felt shiver right down to her toes. He removed his hand and stood back to let her pass. 'After a challenge like that, Faith, you've simply got to let me try.'

With the run of the dice with her and her determination to show him, the first game quickly went her way. After that she found it increasingly difficult to concentrate. The library seemed too quiet, the denseness of its atmosphere absorbing even the clatter of the counters across the inlaid wood.

The world seemed to be slowing

down, and the fading light of the long summer evening had a misty quality, like candlelight, shimmering off the facets of the crystal goblet standing at her elbow, shimmering off the dark, silky hair on Harry's sinewy forearm which flexed as he tossed the dice, shimmering over the harsh planes of his face, throwing the deep hollows at his cheeks and temples into darkest shadow as he looked up from the board.

'It's your throw.'

'Sorry, I was miles away.'

'With your missionary?' Harry looked up. 'How long have you known him?'

Known him? A dangerous question. When Julian had written to the bank with very specific instructions about the arrangements for his investment fund his letter had been passed to her. The correspondence had started formally when she had suggested suitable companies for his portfolio. He had not been prepared to take her word. He had wanted to know the details of her background research.

It was unusual for someone to be quite so interested in her work and she had willingly told him all she could, asking him in turn about his own work. She knew nothing about Antarctica. His enthusiasm had burned off the pages of his reply; it had seemed only kind to send him a Christmas card, which he had noticed was printed on recycled paper. He sent a photograph, all dark goggles and parka. She'd sent him one of her sitting at her desk, and asked for something that gave a clue as to what he actually looked like, but to send it to her flat as the other investment consultants were beginning to tease her . . .

She swallowed, her throat tighter than it should be. No, she wasn't about to tell Harry that she had never actually met her husband-to-be. He wasn't really interested, simply attempting to disturb her concentration. 'Julian, as you very well know, is not a missionary,' she declared. 'And I've . . . um . . . known him for three years.'

'Three years? As long as that?' He

seemed surprised. 'Then why all the sudden rush to get married?'

'Three years is hardly a rush,' she countered, made a stupid move and Harry immediately blocked the corner.

'You won't have seen him for some time, then?'

Faith peered at him from beneath her lashes but was unable to detect anything measured or deliberate about his query. 'No,' she agreed, hoping her voice was steadier than her heartbeat. 'I haven't.'

'Reduced to an exchange of passionate letters.'

'An exchange of letters,' she agreed carefully.

'No passion? No, well, if you're not in love . . . ' He didn't expect or want an answer but threw the dice and mopped up the game. 'You seem to have let that one slip, Faith. I don't believe you're concentrating.'

'No,' she agreed. 'Shall we leave it at that — an honourable draw?'

Harry sat back in his chair and

regarded her thoughtfully. 'I never play percentages, Faith. All or nothing. Win or lose.' There was an intensity about his eyes which held her momentarily transfixed. Were they still talking about backgammon?

'It's only a game, Harry,' she said a little shakily. He didn't answer and she dredged up a casual shrug from the depths of that self-possession for which until two days ago she had been so renowned but which seemed to be rapidly deserting her. 'Of course, if you're determined to be beaten I'll be happy to oblige. One game to settle it? I'm sure I have a countermove to every move you make.' She began to set the pieces but he caught her hand, held it between his own.

'That's a dangerous assumption, Faith.'

'Dangerous? You don't frighten me.' Her voice wasn't as steady as she would have liked, but to prove her point she made no effort to remove her fingers from his, despite the unsettling tingle set off by his touch. At least, she thought that that was why she left her hand resting in his.

'Then on your head be it.'

She looked up. 'What is that supposed to mean?'

'It was your challenge.' His smile was bland, uncommunicative. 'You tell me.'

She drew her forehead down in a tiny frown. 'It's just a game, Harry — ' she began.

'But a game without rules.'

'Don't be silly, of course there are rules.'

His smiled deepened. 'Then why don't you tell me what countermove is appropriate for this move?'

'Countermove?' She was beginning to sound feebleminded, she thought, then caught her breath as he lifted her fingers to his lips, lightly kissing each one in turn. The room seemed to have shrunk to a tiny circle of light in which the two of them confronted each other through an atmosphere supercharged with tension.

'Countermove,' he murmured back at her. 'Response, check, foil, antidote.'

Then, regarding her from beneath lowered lids, Harry March took his mouth on a tour down the length of her thumb, then traced her heart line across the palm of her hand. *Was* there an antidote for Harry March, Faith wondered dizzily? Or was his attraction quite fatal? 'Well?' he prompted softly, and looked up. His mouth was a sensuous curve that offered . . . what? A dare, perhaps? Yes, it was there in his eyes — the merest hint of a challenge that warned her that this *was* only a game, an extension of the lively clash on the backgammon board. So that was all right. Wasn't it?

A quiver of something ran through her. Something that should have been relief, because Faith had always been good at games, especially the kind of game that demanded a long memory and quick wits. Attack and counter-attack. Take your opponent by surprise. What kind of retaliation would he be expecting? A slap, perhaps? No. If she slapped him it would show that it mattered. So, no response, then. Nothing.

It took every ounce of self-control to withdraw her hand as if nothing had happened. 'It's my first throw, I believe.' Her voice was low, very calm. It was quite a performance, considering that her insides were dancing a tango. But she couldn't trust herself to meet his eyes.

'No, leave it,' Harry said abruptly, rising to his feet, sending the counters clattering across the polished wood. 'It's too late for games.'

The relief that rippled through her limbs made her temporarily weak. All she wanted was to get out of the library, away from Harry to the safety of her room. She stumbled to her feet as he pulled back her chair, and he reached out to steady her.

'Faith?' His query was too gentle. 'Look, I'm sorry . . . ' His arm was about her and he tensed at the tremor of excitement that rippled through her body at his touch. Then he swore softly. 'No, I'm not,' he said, his eyes darkening. 'I knew I was right.'

'Harry!' But her protest was too late as his mouth teased across her lips and, infinitely tender, infinitely determined, stole away her senses — stole her level-headed, rational, down-to-earth senses and sent them spinning, tipping, flying like a child's wooden top. She had no idea how long they remained in that intoxicating embrace, how long they would have stayed there, hearts beating in unison, if he had not drawn back so that, without warning, without her even knowing how it had happened, she was a foot away from him, her trembling body held upright only by his hands grasping her shoulders, and she was staring, confused and uncertain, into Harry's shadowed face.

'Some countermove,' he said, his voice a harsh drawl that mocked them both. Heat suffused her cheeks as, furiously, Faith opened her mouth to contradict that brazen statement, deny it with her last breath. Then she snapped it shut. Just in case he should decide to take her into his arms and prove his point beyond any doubt.

'I should have slapped you,' she said, too breathlessly.

'Perhaps you should ask yourself why you didn't.' His grasp tightened slightly, his fingers biting into her shoulders.

'It's not too late,' she warned.

'Yes, it is, darling. Far too late.' And he laughed softly as he released her and quite deliberately stood back to let her by.

For a moment she came close to proving just how wrong he could be, but common sense, prompted by a suspicion of amusement in those dark blue eyes, asserted itself just in time and she clenched her hands tightly to keep them from doing anything stupid. 'Goodnight, Harry,' she said, sweeping by him with as much dignity as she could gather around her.

'Goodnight, Faith. Sweet dreams.'

'I never dream,' she said.

'Not even of your missionary?'

'Never,' she avowed fervently, and

shut the library door firmly behind her before wondering if, under the circumstances, such a declaration had been quite wise.

★　★　★

Faith woke suddenly from a restless, uncomfortable sleep, one moment wrestling hopelessly with some undefined problem, the next totally awake and listening, knowing that something had woken her but uncertain of the cause. Then the noise was repeated. Harry's little box of tricks was letting her know that Ben was awake and unhappy. She sighed and sat up, pushing her hair back from her face before swinging her feet to the floor. A light had been left burning in the hall and, shivering slightly in the cool night air, she padded along to the children's room. Alice hadn't stirred, but Ben was wet and fed up and didn't care who knew about it.

He stopped crying when she picked him up and changed him, and then

162

looked at her, his eyes not quite focused, his head a little wobbly. 'What's the matter, sweetheart?' she asked gently, picking him up again, her cheek resting lightly on his downy head, and crooned softly to him as he drifted off to sleep against her shoulder.

A movement caught her eye and she turned. Harry, a silk dressing gown thrown about him, was watching her from the doorway, totally absorbed by the tender scene of a young woman with a baby in her arms. Their eyes met briefly and for a moment Faith thought he was about to say something, then his jaw clamped tight and he turned and walked away without a word.

6

As they approached the bridal shop the following morning, Alice tugged at her hand and pointed to a frilly concoction in candyfloss-pink net in the corner of the window. 'That one, Faith!' she declared fervently. 'Can I have that one?'

Faith didn't dare look at Harry. He had not mentioned their silent night-time encounter, had been in an odd mood ever since their paths had crossed in the kitchen not long after six. Maybe he had been looking forward to another display of the red silk pyjamas, although she'd noticed that he had pulled on his jogging pants before making his own appearance. But she had taken care to dress before she'd ventured from her room.

'I could take Alice into Melchester,' she offered, more in hope than expectation, 'if you would look after Ben.'

'And miss all the fun?'

And that had been that. She'd assumed that he intended to encourage his niece in her outrageous taste in frocks, but he made no comment on Alice's choice.

'Why don't you wait and try some on before you decide, Alice?' Faith advised, taking her hand and leading her through the door. 'They'll have heaps more dresses to choose from inside.'

'You'll need time to choose your own dress,' Harry reminded her coolly. 'The missionary will be expecting something virginal and white, I imagine?'

She didn't answer. It was the first indication that he had even remembered their kiss but he couldn't have made his thoughts plainer. No eager bride-to-be would have reacted as she had, and if he hadn't called a halt . . .

Her embarrassment was total, as was her shame, redoubling her determination to leave the choice of a wedding dress until she was safely back in London. This morning was going to be devoted entirely to dressing Alice and, to that end, she hoped the child would be extremely difficult to please. Even tantrums would be welcome and she hoped Ben would scream blue murder. Anything would be preferable to donning snow-white lace for the cynical amusement of Mr Harry March.

The elegant woman who approached them, however, was hijacked by Harry. All it took was a smile and she was putty in his hands. Faith knew the feeling and sympathised. 'We're looking for a dress for Alice.'

'That's me,' Alice said, just to make sure the lady understood. 'I'm going to be a flower girl and I like the pink dress in the window,' she added with determination.

The saleswoman caught the slight shake of Faith's head. 'Are there any other attendants?' she asked.

'The adult bridesmaids are wearing ivory and green,' Faith said gratefully.

'Something like that.' She indicated a dress displayed on a dummy.

'Ah, yes. They've been very popular this year.' Faith could not resist throwing Harry a sideways look before bending over the buggy to wipe away a dribble from Ben's mouth. 'And the bride? Is her dress ivory too?'

'She'll be choosing her dress today,' Harry replied, with nerve-racking determination.

Startled, the woman turned to Faith. 'Madam is the bride?'

Harry smiled. 'Madam is the bride,' he agreed.

'I see.' The woman heroically refrained from looking at the children but blinked several times rather quickly. 'Ivory, perhaps, would be . . . more appropriate.'

'Appropriate?' Harry tested the word. 'What do you say, Faith? Do you think ivory would be more appropriate?'

She favoured him with a withering glance, but infuriatingly he refused to be withered so she turned her attention to Alice. 'Let's concentrate on one thing at a time, shall we?'

Alice, faced with a selection of the most beribboned and frilled dresses she had ever seen, was in seventh heaven as she paraded for them in a delicate array of satin and lace. The three of them finally decided upon an enchanting cream voile dress scattered with tiny peach silk rosebuds. Satin slippers, fine matching tights and a tiny circle of peach silk rosebuds for her dark hair completed the ensemble and were borne away by a junior to be packed. It had been easy. Too easy, she thought as Harry turned to her.

'Now it's your turn.'

'No. I'll take ages and the children are getting fractious . . . ' But Ben lay fast asleep in his buggy. No help from that quarter.

'It won't take any time at all,' Harry said, smiling with the confidence of a man who knew he had won. He nodded to a gown on display. 'I've already decided on that one.'

'You've *what*?'

The saleswoman cleared her throat. 'The groom really shouldn't see the dress before the wedding,' she said. 'It's considered unlucky.'

'That's all right,' Harry replied. 'Faith isn't superstitious. Are you, darling?'

Faith glared at him. 'Since you aren't the groom it wouldn't matter even if I were,' she retaliated, before following the saleswoman, who was all blushing apology as she led the way to the display of gowns.

'I'm so sorry — '

'I'm not. Not in the least bit sorry,' said Faith, with more force than was entirely necessary, and drew a curious look from the woman. She turned away quickly to look at the dress Harry had picked. It was an off-the-shoulder extravagance with a tiny lace bodice, puffed shoulders and bows scattered along the length of the train.

'It is lovely, isn't it? Your . . . um . . . friend has an excellent eye. It really would suit you.'

The dress *was* beautiful, with simple, elegant lines that emphasised the richness of the fabric. Under different circumstances she would have tried it on without a murmur, but she wasn't giving Harry the satisfaction of seeing her try on something he had chosen. He was having quite enough amusement at her expense already. 'I'm looking for something simple,' Faith said, before the woman could get into her stride. 'Something plain . . .'

'I thought you already had that,' Harry murmured, and she turned, the slightest frown creasing her brow. 'Julian Fellowes?'

'Very funny. Why don't you do something useful, like taking Alice to buy her the red pyjamas you promised for her birthday?'

Alice, blessed child, didn't need prompting twice to set up a clamour, and Faith breathed a sigh of relief as they left the store, leaving Ben in the adoring charge of one of the assistants. 'I'm looking for something simple,' she repeated. But the simple gowns with demure portrait collars made her look far too much like the bride of some nineteenth-century missionary and she knew Harry wouldn't hesitate to say so. Not that it was any of his business. 'I think I'd better leave it,' she said as she stared unhappily at her reflection. 'I don't think I'm in the mood to buy a wedding dress.'

But the saleswoman wasn't about to lose a valuable customer. 'Why not try something different?' she suggested.

Faith, who would have done anything to get out of the shop, agreed with the proviso that it would have to be the last one. 'The children will be fretting for their lunch,' she explained.

'Your friend isn't back yet. Look, let me bring you some underwear first. The dress I have in mind needs something strapless underneath it.' Not that the delicate lace basque she produced could be described as prosaically as mere *underwear*, Faith decided, regarding her reflection in the mirror. The lace

171

looked as virginal as any groom might have wished. The effect was anything but. Then the dress Harry had chosen was carried in by an assistant.

'Oh, no . . . ' Faith began. The woman simply smiled and waited. It was beautiful. Stupid not to try it just because Harry had chosen it, and if she was quick he need never know. Unless he brought Alice to the wedding, her subconscious pointed out. But he wouldn't. His sister would be back from America and she would bring Alice . . . And anyway the whole question was academic, because as the gown was settled over her and the tiny buttons fastened into place down the back she knew she had to have it.

'It could have been made for you,' the saleswoman said as she stood up from straightening the train and admired her handiwork. 'Like something from a fairy tale.'

'If you believe in fairy tales.' And suddenly, regarding her reflection in the mirror, she had to blink back the sting of a tear. She and Michael had been pure fairy tale. She had worshipped him as a gawky teenager, lived in a nightmare of anxiety for the holidays, when he'd come home from university. Would he bring a girl home? Would he even notice her existence? Then suddenly she had been free of braces, had developed the necessary curves and he had finally noticed her. More than noticed her. She had believed in fairy tales then and had bought a dress bedecked with as many frills as could have been wished for . . .

But she and Julian had nothing to do with such nonsense. Although he had left all the arrangements to her, she suspected that he would have preferred a simple register-office ceremony. She would have preferred it herself after the trauma of being jilted by Michael, but the dress and the church were customs that had to be respected when your father was a clergyman and she knew he would understand.

'Isn't it too long?' she asked a little

brusquely. It seemed necessary to find some fault, some reason to reject perfection.

'Maybe an inch. Easily fixed. I'll pin it for you.' The woman swept back the curtain and suddenly Faith was standing in full view of the room.

Ben was asleep in his buggy. Alice was 'helping' one of the younger assistants. Harry was sitting on a small gilt chair, tipping it back, eyes half-closed apparently in boredom. At the swish of the curtain, the whisper of silk, his chair dropped back to the carpet and he looked up. Then he rose to his feet, and for a long time it seemed to Faith that the room was intensely quiet.

Then he nodded. 'You're quite right, Faith,' he said very softly, after an age during which his eyes had devoured her slightly flushed cheeks, her smooth golden shoulders, the soft swell of a bosom that rose and fell a little too rapidly. 'That dress is far too good to waste on a man who counts penguins for a living.'

174

That hurt. Only the sudden loss of colour from her cheeks betrayed how much it hurt as Faith met his unwavering stare head-on. 'But the dress was your choice, Harry,' she retaliated. 'I thought you would be pleased.' She glanced down at the woman, who was on her knees preparing to pin the hem. 'Will it take long to have it altered? The wedding is in three weeks.'

'Only a day or two. It's not a busy time of year.' She glanced up, saw the look that passed like daggers between the bride and the man she was *not* going to marry and wondered . . . 'What kind of heels will you be wearing?'

'Heels?'

'You're quite tall, and with a headdress . . . Will you be wearing high heels?'

Faith glanced down at the woman's upturned face. 'Oh. Not too high.' Harry made a small disgusted noise which she ignored. 'I'm not very comfortable in high heels,' she added firmly, almost believing it. The truth was that Julian was only a couple of inches taller than she was. If she had been marrying Harry it would have been different. She could have got away with stilts.

She caught herself. What on earth was she thinking about? Harry had already jilted one woman. She'd been there herself. Knew the pain. He was the last man on earth ... 'Perhaps I should try some on while I'm wearing the dress?' She forced a smile to her lips. 'You don't mind, do you, Harry? I might as well buy everything at the same time. In fact I'd be glad of your help, since you have such good taste.'

'Please, take all the time you need,' he replied, with the grace of a man who knew he had had his bluff called but was confident that he would be able to exact retribution in his own good time. Faith told herself that she didn't care. Sarah Downes would be firmly in charge of the nursery by evening and she would be safely in London by nightfall. Harry March could do his worst, but she would exact payment in advance.

She took her time, choosing shoes then a headdress and a shoulder-length veil, each time turning to Harry, demanding his approval, taking perverse pleasure in the fact that his temper seemed to deteriorate with every purchase.

'I think that's everything,' she said, when she thought that Harry had learned his lesson and had been kept waiting long enough. She should have known better.

'Aren't you going to choose the rest of your trousseau?' he asked. 'This store has some of the most beautiful lingerie I've ever seen.'

'And I'm sure you've seen plenty in your time,' she muttered, under her breath.

'I've had my moments,' he replied, reminding her that his hearing was as acute as his mind. 'What about this?' he asked, taking a suspender belt, the barest scrap of white lace, from a display and offering it for her inspection. 'I'm quite certain that Julian would really like this.'

'You have no idea what Julian would

like . . . ' He didn't bother to argue. He simply twanged the suspender, leaving his eyes to do all the talking. Faith swallowed hard. 'Besides . . . it would be a little flimsy to wear for trekking across icy wastes in search of penguins, wouldn't you say?'

His eyes gleamed. 'Wear something like this — ' he indicated another item ' — and I'm sure Julian Fellowes could be persuaded to forget all about penguins.' 'This' was a scrap of lace that might have been a pair of pants. Well, no, hardly a *pair*. 'Or this?' He held a slinky black satin nightgown against her, the knuckles of his hand grazing her throat.

But for Harry the joke had worn so thin that she could see through it. 'Black's a little obvious, isn't it?' she asked, jerking away from the smooth feel of the cloth which raised goose-flesh on her skin. From the hard touch of his knuckles against her throat.

'I don't think you could be obvious if you tried.' His mouth twisted in a provocative little smile. 'But they have it in red if you prefer . . . '

'In red?' Something snapped inside her and she turned to the saleswoman. 'I'll take them both.'

'There are matching wraps . . . ' the woman urged, sensing a crackle in the atmosphere that could only be good for business.

'I'll take them as well,' Faith said without hesitation. Turning back to the rack, she swept her eyes along it in search of inspiration. It was provided by a black satin teddy. 'Do you think this is obvious?'

She didn't wait for his reply but moved along the rows of deliciously lace-encrusted lingerie, choosing the slinkiest, the sexiest pieces she could find. French knickers, teddies, slips . . . It was reckless; it was stupid. It was worth it just to see the look on Harry March's face as she turned to him with a flimsy black lace basque. 'Well, Harry?' she demanded.

He didn't answer.

'Come along, don't be shy. Give me

the benefit of all your worldly experience. What do you think about this? Will Julian like it?'

'Do you really want to know what I think?' Harry's eyes had lost the teasing sparkle that had driven her over the edge. They were dark now — slaty dark and angry.

'No, Harry . . . ' Rapidly abandoning the provocative posture she had adopted, Faith surrendered the basque to the saleswoman, who, realising that the impulsive raid on her lingerie department was over, moved tactfully out of earshot. 'I'm not in the least bit interested in what you think.' She made a move to follow the saleswoman, but he seized her arm, his touch jarring through her like a bolt of lightning — frighteningly intense, intensely frightening. He saw it, felt her reaction and eased his grip slightly.

'I'll tell you anyway. I don't know why you're marrying Julian Fellowes, but by your own admission you're not in love with him — '

'Love? What would you know about

love?' she grated, furious that she had allowed him to taunt her into making such a fool of herself. All she wanted to do was escape from this shop, escape from him, but he hadn't finished with her and he wasn't about to let her go until he had quite done.

'More than you, that's certain.'

'I know that romantic love is for silly girls who know no better.'

'I don't believe you.'

'Harry . . . '

But he ignored the warning in her voice. 'I might have,' he conceded, 'if I hadn't just been treated to a demonstration of just how dizzy you can be when provoked. I might have fallen for your own public relations but I'm beginning to hope that there's a chance for you yet.'

'No!' Faith lifted her head, threw a wild gesture in the direction of the lingerie racks. 'It . . . it was just a joke — '

'A joke?' His laughter was hollow. 'You might be able to fool yourself, Faith, but you can't fool me. You were reacting — just like you reacted last night when I kissed you — all heart and no head — '

'No!'

'You don't like that? You prefer to be buttoned up, in control?' He shrugged. 'Well, no doubt emotions are easier to deal with at long distance, through the post. It won't be quite so easy when you're tucked up in a big double bed, in your red silk nightdress with — '

Her eyes flew wide, her cheeks coloured furiously. 'Stop it, Harry!' she demanded.

Harry instantly released her, raising his hands to demonstrate his obedience to her command. 'With a man you don't love,' he finished quietly. Then his mouth twisted in a wry smile. 'Tell me, Faith, do you think 'Stop it, *Julian*' will be as effective, considering your man's been away in the Antarctic for . . . how long?'

It was Ben who saved her — beautiful Ben, waking up, demanding to be picked up and cuddled — and Faith was his grateful and willing slave, cradling him in her arms and crooning softly to him as she buried her face in his soft dark curls.

'Cuddle *me*, Uncle Harry,' Alice demanded fretfully, clinging to his legs.

For a moment he continued to regard Faith with an odd little expression that made her feel even worse. Then he bent and picked up Alice and she burrowed her head into his shoulder. 'Come on, Faith. It's time to go home.'

'I'll have to wait . . . ' She gestured helplessly at the piles of frothy under-garments.

But apparently Harry had had enough. 'You can deliver everything with the dress,' he said, handing a card to the assistant.

'No . . . ' Faith's protest was ignored, and with his free hand firmly at her back he propelled her towards the door. 'But I'm going home — '

'Yes,' he agreed curtly. 'Right now.' She didn't pursue his deliberate misunderstanding, vowing silently to sort it out later. Only when they'd reached the Range Rover and had fastened the children into their restraints did he break the silence as he helped her up onto the high seat. 'Tell me, Faith,' he asked quietly, 'what *did* make you buy all that rather dizzy lingerie? It doesn't quite fit the image of the practical, efficient banker . . . '

She busied herself with her seat belt. 'Even bankers wear knickers,' she declared.

'French ones?' She lifted her head to glare at him, too late catching the gleam of mischief in his eyes.

'What else?' she enquired, refusing to give an inch.

'You'd have done better spending your money on something sensible, like thermals. Long johns, vests — that sort of thing. You can get them in silk; I've seen them in — '

'I've got all the underwear I need,' she told him sharply. 'And a great deal more, thanks to you.'

'To me? I'd like to think so. I

couldn't have picked a more entertaining selection if I were marrying you myself. Although perhaps Julian won't much appreciate it as an explanation for wearing a *black* nightdress on your wedding night. Or even a red one, come to that.'

'I don't want to talk about underwear, Harry.'

'Don't you? You were eager enough for my opinion a minute or two ago.'

Faith didn't reply. It wasn't that the words weren't right there, on the tip of her tongue, doing their suicidal best to leap off. But she kept her mouth clamped shut because everything she said seemed to make things worse.

Thermal underwear indeed! As if Julian would expect her to live in a hut within hailing distance of the South Pole! He had been offered a post at Cambridge University and she was going to start her own financial consultancy for people who wanted to be certain of the moral probity of the companies they invested their money with.

Harry, however, refused to take the hint. 'Well, I don't suppose that flimsy stuff will be entirely wasted. He must be planning to take you somewhere warm for your honeymoon. An igloo would be a bit daunting, even with a double sleeping bag.'

'I can't think why you're so concerned, Harry.' It took a supreme effort to answer him in a coolly dismissive tone. 'Besides, I'm sure you're perfectly well aware that igloos are *Arctic* dwellings. That's the *North* Pole, you know . . . ' She gave an exclamation of disgust as she realised that once again she had fallen into his teasing trap. All she had to do was stop rising to his bait like a hungry trout and he would stop.

A few more hours, she promised herself. Just a few more hours and then she would be free to concentrate on her own affairs. On her wedding. To Julian.

Harry glanced at her. 'What's the matter?'

'Matter?' She glanced at him, uncertain what new torment he was planning.

'You sighed.'

'I didn't!'

'You know you did. I can't say I blame you. Marriage is a perilous adventure even when you're in love. Since you're not . . . ' He left her to draw her own conclusions, but she refused to play his game of tease-the-bride any more. It had gone quite far enough.

'Aunt Janet always said you were an adventurous boy. I wouldn't have thought you were the kind to chicken out of any adventure, particularly a perilous one.'

He stopped at a set of lights and turned to her, the scar across his forehead puckering as he drew his brows together. He lifted his hand in an unconscious gesture and rubbed absently at the cicatrice. 'Janet said a damned sight too much.' Faith glanced warningly at him, but the children were both fast asleep. 'And I didn't chicken out.'

'No? I rather think that Clementine Norwood should be the judge of that,' she said with considerable feeling.

'Do you? You seem to take my desertion of her very personally. I wonder why?'

If she took it personally it was because she knew how Clementine must have felt. Harry had undoubtedly been her hero too. It was a role he had played to the hilt . . . Harry continued to stare at her until, increasingly uncomfortable, she said, 'Your sister hasn't given up hope of finding you another victim.'

Her choice of words clearly startled him, but a hoot from behind forced his attention back to the road. Once they were moving he returned to the subject. 'I'm not looking for a victim, Faith. Elizabeth thinks it's my duty to provide Ben and Alice with some cousins. And not to take too long about it.'

'So *that's* why she torments you with doe-eyed blondes. How shockingly selfish of her,' Faith replied, her tongue firmly in her cheek, yet certain that Elizabeth had her brother's well-being closer to her heart than that. Not that he deserved it. She was sure he knew it too, although whether he would ever admit it was another matter entirely.

'It doesn't matter. Most of them take one look and flee.' It was her turn to be startled and his brows rose, mocking her shocked expression. '*Beauty and the Beast* is a fairy tale, Faith. Reality is somewhat different.'

'You might not be a beauty, Harry, and you're certainly the most irritating man I've ever met, but you're hardly a beast.'

'You have a refreshingly frank line in compliments, Faith.'

'You're entirely welcome.' She regarded him carefully from beneath lowered lids, wondering what it must be like to have everything, to be the top of the heap when it came to the kind of looks that made every girl turn her head and want to be with you, bear your children, and then to lose it all. Except he hadn't lost it. Surely he must know that? For heaven's sake, she'd very nearly swooned in his arms . . .

Her lips seemed to burn as she remembered just how it felt to be kissed by Harry March. Even now she wanted to reach out and soothe the scar tissue, hold him, give him endless cousins for Alice and Ben . . . Horrified, she snapped her gaze away to stare straight ahead through the windscreen. 'What happened?' she asked.

His sharp glance warned her that not many were brave enough to ask. 'Didn't *Aunt Janet* tell you that?' he demanded sarcastically.

'No. Why should she?'

'She seems to have told you everything else.'

'She simply told me you were the most *determined* bachelor she had ever met.'

'And Elizabeth has persuaded her that she ought to help her do something about it?'

'I've no idea, but since I'm getting married to Julian in three weeks' time I'm hardly a suitable candidate to dish out the tea and sympathy.'

'I'm not looking for sympathy.'

'I've never met a man who needed it less.' She turned and for a second their eyes clashed, then Faith shook her head quickly. 'For heaven's sake, Harry, if only perfect specimens made it the human race would have died out a long time ago. Marriage is about more than that. There's a line in the service about 'mutual society, help, and comfort'.'

His response was short and to the point. 'Tell me, Faith, are you getting married, or forming the Faith and Julian Fellowes Mutual Friendly Society?'

'That sounds like the basis for an ideal marriage to me,' she replied, stonily refusing to dwell on what *he* might consider to be an ideal union.

'No, it damned well doesn't. It sounds like a building society, for heaven's sake, and about as exciting.'

She blinked rapidly, shaken by the vehemence of his response. 'Well,' she said, with a very small attempt at a laugh as they pulled up in front of the manor,

'I'm a banker. Remember?'

'I hadn't forgotten. But perhaps it's time you remembered that you're a woman first. Where's the romance, Faith? Where's the white heat of passion?'

'Romance? Passion?' she demanded, too loudly in the sudden silence. She glanced anxiously back at the children but they were both still asleep. She dropped her voice to an angry whisper. 'Who needs them?'

'We all do.' Harry March sat back, propping his elbow on the back of his seat as he reached forward to tuck a stray strand of hair behind her ear. His fingers were cool against her throbbing temple and she shivered, just a little. 'Last night I proved that.'

'That's not fair.'

'All's fair in love and war. I carry the scars to prove it.'

'And so does Clemmie Norwood.'

'I warned you that this was a game without rules, Faith.' He leaned across her, so that she was enveloped in the heady male scent of him, his arm brushing for a tantalising moment against her, and she held herself rigid, expecting him to kiss her, sweep her away on a tide of white-hot passion to prove his point.

For one heady moment she wanted him to do just that. But he didn't. Instead he released her seat belt. Then, as he straightened, he paused and looked straight into her eyes. 'It's a lot more exciting than backgammon, I promise you.'

7

Excitement. As Faith cradled Ben she could still feel the edge of it, the dangerous draw of the passion Harry had trailed as a lure. It shivered deep within her, stirring up long-suppressed desires, the ache of longing deep within her. It had been so long since she had been held, kissed, loved. She had been wearing her career, wearing Julian like shields, but they were no defence against a man like Harry March. He made her skin tingle, her pulse beat far too quickly. He made her feel . . . alive.

A tear fell on Ben's cheek, making him jump and wave his tiny hands anxiously. She wiped it gently away with the tip of her finger, kissed his forehead, murmuring softly to him.

She hadn't thought it possible to cry any more tears over Michael. But perhaps the tear wasn't for him. Maybe it was for herself, for all the wasted years while she had kept her distance, refusing the invitations that had come her way, using any excuse not to become involved again, hurt again, while her friends fell in love, married, had babies. And divorced, she reminded herself. Some of them. Too many of them. It could have happened to her if she had married Michael. At eighteen she had been far too young for marriage. Easy to think that now, with the vastly superior hindsight of a twenty-five-year-old.

She hadn't always been so objective, so level-headed. At eighteen she had been too giddy with the excitement of love to consider anything but happy-ever-after. When she had opened Michael's letter it had been as if she had hit a brick wall as she was thrown off the merry-go-round. Harry might mock her, but she wouldn't willingly put herself through that again.

Her marriage to Julian wouldn't be based on such insubstantial emotions but on respect, compatibility, shared ideals. It might not have the giddy highs of passion and romance, but it wouldn't have the painful lows either. And if her family and friends weren't quite convinced it was because they hadn't thought about it as carefully as she had.

She dropped a kiss on Ben's dark, downy curls. He grinned gummily up at her, squeezing her heart, so that for a dangerous moment her breath caught in her throat. She had always wanted babies. She and Michael had planned to have at least four . . . She stiffened. *She* had planned to have at least four . . . Babies were for women, their consolation as love turned to routine. She and Julian would be too busy for that. She would have no need of consolation, and if no babies was the price she had to pay for peace of heart, well, so be it.

She lifted the warm infant to her shoulder. 'And as for Harry March,' she murmured softly to him, 'what would an irritable old beast of a bachelor know about such things?'

'Do you often chat to babies?'

'Ben's a great listener and he doesn't answer back,' Faith replied, wondering if Harry had seen her jump, or whether she just imagined that she had left the chair. He was leaning against the doorframe, so at ease that she had the uncomfortable feeling that he had been watching her for some time. Had he noticed the tears? 'Where's Alice?' she asked quickly. 'Playing with her kitten?' He'd taken her to fetch it after lunch — an enchanting scrap of creamy fur with the promise of a chocolate face and paws.

'No, the poor little thing needed a rest so I'm taking Alice for a swim. She's decided that she wants to be able to swim a length of the pool before her mother comes home.'

'Your idea, no doubt.' Faith looked thoughtfully at the baby. 'I wonder if Ben would like the water?'

'Elizabeth takes him in most days when she's staying. Will you join us?'

The idea of a swim was appealing, but the thought of sharing the pool with Harry was not. He possessed more unbridled masculinity than even the most level-headed girl could handle if he chose to exert it. She had responded unashamedly to his kiss and would be a fool if she believed he wouldn't take advantage of the situation.

'I thought you insisted on having the pool to yourself. I can take Ben in later . . . '

'Since you've already seen the mess I made of my leg and were kind enough to refrain from actually fainting — '

'I don't faint and, besides, I've seen far worse . . . '

'Have you indeed?'

Well, that wasn't very clever, Faith, she chided herself as his eyes darkened ominously.

'What a very interesting life you must lead at that bank,' he said coldly, and turned to go. 'Elizabeth left a couple of costumes at the pool, if you need one,' he added as an afterthought.

'I have my own.'

'Of course, I remember — you swim every day at your club. Well, I'm sorry I can't offer you more congenial company.'

And that apparently was that. She fetched her swimming bag from the boot of her car then followed the path that Harry and Alice had taken. The pool was in its own building beyond the walled garden. From the front it still looked like the carriage house it had once been but, inside, Faith saw that this was simply a façade. It had been stripped out and the far wall, overlooking the manor's parkland, had been largely removed and replaced with a wall of glass that slid back, so that during a warm spell bathers could walk out onto a terrace and relax in the sun on the old cane recliners that had been carried out there.

The remainder of the interior had been clad in pine and at the far end there were changing rooms and a sauna. But the pool dominated everything — pale blue, in a broad frame of the beautiful terracotta tiles that continued, without a break, onto the terrace.

'This is a serious swimming pool,' Faith said, a little lost for words. She had been expecting something smaller. Much smaller.

Harry shrugged. 'My surgeon suggested I swim to exercise my leg. I thought if I had anything smaller I'd be at the end before I'd done more than two strokes.'

'Did you? How close did you come to drowning before you discovered your mistake?'

He gave her a sharp glance. 'What would you know about it?'

'Boys who climb down drainpipes don't change their nature just because they grow a metre, Harry.'

The tenseness left his face as he responded to her teasing with an ironic little twist of his mouth that might have been a smile. If it was, he was laughing at himself. 'Perhaps not. Just as well Mac appointed himself as my guardian angel. But you didn't answer my question.'

Faith shrugged. 'I used to help a local

physiotherapist run swimming sessions for accident victims. Most men misjudge how weak they'll be after a long spell in bed.'

'Used to?'

'At home, before I moved to London.' It had been part of the good works her father had prescribed to dull the heartache. She had enjoyed it; it had passed the time. As for the heartache . . . 'I rather miss it.' She didn't wait to gauge his reaction but escaped to the changing room.

She emerged a few minutes later with Ben in her arms, ridiculously self-conscious in a clinging black suit that at her club had always seemed sober and workmanlike but now felt as if it was cut provocatively low across her breasts.

Alice and Harry, however, were working along the length of the pool and they appeared not to notice her as she waded down the steps at the shallow end. The water was blissfully warm and Ben gurgled happily, splashing with his hands, and as she grew in confidence with him she laid him on her stomach and began to swim backwards, kicking her feet, holding him lightly so that he could float free and kick his little legs. She was brought to an abrupt halt by a pair of strong hands seizing her shoulders.

'You were running out of pool,' Harry said, his head and shoulders disconcertingly upside down.

'I was just about to turn around.'

'Of course you were,' he said, grinning down at her.

'Where's Alice?' she demanded.

'Drying herself. Here, let me help.' Before she could right herself, she felt his body rise beneath hers and take her weight. Then he began to swim with her back down the pool, just as she had been swimming with Ben. Her back was lying against his broad chest and she could feel his coarse dark hair against her skin. His hands were at her waist. The lightest touch, nothing to scream about. But she wanted to scream as his legs tangled with hers, had to bite down on her lip to keep the sound from escaping as the unaccustomed ache of longing swept over her, and she was grateful for Ben who stopped her from turning in the water to lay her cheek against the rough hair on Harry's chest, entwine her arms about his neck.

As if he knew every treacherous thought that winged through her mind, Harry held her up in the water when she tried to put her feet down and push herself away from him — away from the temptation she was sure was calculated to demonstrate . . . something. She refused to contemplate what. And as he held her he quite deliberately placed a kiss in the angle between her neck and shoulder, knowing that while she had Ben in her arms she was completely at his mercy.

'Passion has its pleasures,' he murmured.

'You'd know more about that than me,' she snapped out from between furious lips. 'Now, if you'll excuse me, Ben has been in the water quite long enough.'

'Here. Let me have him. I'll wrap him up in a towel while you work off all that pent-up aggression.' He stood up and scooped Ben off her stomach, his eyes sparkling with mischief as they swept the length of her body in a manner that made her blush. 'Cool off, Faith,' he ordered, 'before you explode.' Before she could move he had put his hand flat on the middle of her chest and ducked her. She came up spluttering with rage to confront his grinning countenance.

'You . . . you . . . '

'You wouldn't hit a man holding a baby, would you?'

Words failed her. She turned and plunged beneath the surface and didn't come up again until she was halfway down the pool. Then she began to swim fast up and down the length of it. But, no matter how hard she drove her body through the water, she couldn't shake off the memory of Harry's touch at her waist, his body beneath her. It clung to her like a forbidden pleasure, and he was right — she was ready to explode. Every time he looked at her or touched her, it seemed to raise the stakes, obliterating the lingering pain of Michael's desertion, driving Julian from her mind.

Being level-headed, knowing that romance was nothing but fantasy was scant protection, she decided as she climbed out of the pool and went to the changing room. It was disturbing to discover just how vulnerable she still could be to a determined purveyor of dreams. Was that the reason Janet had sent her into Harry's lair? Did she know that her favourite charge wouldn't be able to resist a challenge, suspect that her only niece was all too vulnerable to the prickly charm of a man who was painfully conscious of his imperfections. Even at short notice she should surely have been able to find a suitable nanny from her vast network of contacts. Could Harry have been right in his first assumption: had Elizabeth and Janet colluded to throw them together?

She stopped towelling her hair. Julian's

last letter was still in the pocket of her bag, with photographs of him and some of the research team. She took them out and looked at them. He was so serious, as if taking the time to smile for the camera was a waste of energy to be saved for more important undertakings. Had he ever made her laugh?

'Faith?' Harry's voice interrupted the uncomfortable thoughts that were crowding in and she quickly jammed the envelope back in the bag before opening the door.

'Yes?'

'I'm taking Alice down to feed the ducks before tea. I thought you might worry if you couldn't find us.' He stooped and picked something up. A photograph. 'Is this yours?' He turned it over, stared at it for a moment. 'Which one is Julian?'

She glanced at the picture. It was of a group of them. They wore parkas, their hoods up against the biting wind; it was impossible to distinguish one man from another. 'Does it matter?' she asked.

Harry looked up. 'Probably not,' he murmured. 'Since you don't love him.'

He returned the photograph, and as he closed the door behind him she heard him summon Alice to his side.

★ ★ ★

To Faith's relief, Sarah Downes arrived just before six, diffusing the electricity in the atmosphere which seemed to be generated whenever she and Harry crossed paths. Sarah brought with her a brisk, down-to-earth common sense that had been singularly lacking in the previous two days, taking over the nursery with an efficiency that left Faith almost breathless with admiration and just a little jealous as she saw the ease with which she captured Ben's little heart, raising delighted squeals as she tickled his tummy.

And Harry didn't flirt with her, she noted somewhat wryly, but treated Sarah as the professional she was. Why on earth couldn't she have managed such detachment? Because, she answered herself wryly, as she cleared up her bedroom, she wasn't detached. She might find him infuriating, tormenting even, but he trailed emotion like a piece of wool offered to a kitten, tempting her to follow wherever he chose to lead her . . . Her fingers lingered on the curve of her neck where his mouth had brushed her skin . . .

She snapped her hand back, folded her jeans and stuffed them into her bag, drawing the zip shut. She was leaving. Right now. She turned and was almost knocked off her feet by Alice, who flung herself at Faith's knees, wrapping her arms about them. 'Don't go, Faith. Please don't leave me,' she sobbed.

'Alice?' She tried to disentangle the child, but she clung like a limpet. 'Sweetheart, whatever is the matter?'

'I don't like *her*!' She flung an arm briefly behind her and Faith looked up to find Sarah standing the doorway with a towel over her arm and a rueful grin on her face. Harry was close behind her, looking absolutely furious.

'Alice, for goodness' sake behave yourself,' he snapped. Faith raised her brows in surprise. He normally had so much patience with the child. 'Faith can't stay and that's that.'

Sarah appeared undisturbed by the scene. 'It's quite understandable, Harry,' she said, making no effort to impose her will on Alice. 'She's missing her parents and now, just as she's become used to Faith, she's going as well . . . ' She raised her eyes to Faith's. 'It's such a pity you have to leave.'

'Faith has pressing business elsewhere,' Harry interjected, with uncharacteristic sharpness. 'Children are not her scene.'

'Oh, but . . . ' Faith began to deny it, then stopped. He was right. She had told him so herself. Disconcerted by the sudden pang of anguish this caused, Faith crouched down beside Alice and put her arms about her. 'Darling, if I don't go home I won't be able to organise my wedding. And if there isn't any wedding you can't be my flower girl and wear that pretty dress . . . '

It made no difference. 'I don't care. I don't want you to go!' The child's voice was rising towards hysteria and her arm tightened in a stranglehold about Faith's neck when Harry tried to remove her.

'If you let Sarah give you a bath, Alice, you can wear your red pyjamas tonight,' Harry promised. 'Instead of having to wait for your birthday.'

'I want Faith to bath me,' Alice replied, refusing to be bought. If she hadn't been so concerned Faith would have applauded her. Too soon. 'Then I'll wear my red pyjamas. Faith can help me put them on.'

'You're a big girl, Alice. You don't need any help,' he pointed out, less than kindly, and the child's face began to crumple again.

'Leave her alone,' Faith said, pulling her closer to comfort her. She couldn't think what had come over Harry. Surely he could see that he was making things worse? And she didn't want to go, for heaven's sake. She didn't have any choice. The words clanged somewhere deep inside her brain. She shouldn't be thinking like that. She should be thinking about Julian, her wedding . . .

'Couldn't you stay for tonight?' Sarah suggested. 'Just before bedtime is always . . . well, difficult . . . '

'I'll stay and see her settled.' She certainly couldn't leave Alice like this. Janet would never forgive her. She'd never forgive herself.

Harry raised a pair of dark sardonic brows. 'I didn't think you could wait to get back to London.' Why did he have to make everything sound like a criticism? 'She has remarkable stamina, as I know to my cost. It might be eight or nine before you can get away.'

A whimper from Ben drew Sarah away and they were left glaring at one another over Alice's head.

He was baiting her; she knew it but could not resist. 'I'm allowed out after dark, Harry.'

'With Julian away?'

'He's been away for three years, Harry . . . ' Her voice died away as his head lifted slightly.

'Love at first sight, was it? There couldn't have been much time for a second glance.' He didn't wait for an answer. 'Oh, no. It couldn't be that because you're not in love. I can't think why you're bothering with marriage at all.'

'It's none of your business.'

'Maybe not, but I'd rather not have to worry about your travelling alone down the motorway at night.'

'You don't have to worry about me at all.'

'Worry isn't something you can switch off at will.' Despite the bite in his voice, she realised that his concern was genuine but preferred not to wonder why. And, truth to tell, after reading about a couple of recent ugly incidents on the motorway she didn't much care for the idea either. She had considered installing a phone in the car, but since she would be selling it soon there hadn't seemed much point.

'I suppose I could leave in the morning . . . It's too late to do anything today and if I leave very early it won't make much difference.' She almost *saw* her subconscious lift its eyebrows at her in a sardonic little sneer equal to anything that Harry could have produced. She ignored it. Sarah was here now and she was free to go any time she wanted. But it wouldn't be fair to leave her with Alice screaming blue murder. Or to leave Alice when she was so obviously unhappy.

'You mustn't allow Alice to blackmail you,' Harry said, just a touch smugly, she thought.

'She doesn't know the meaning of the word. Besides, she can safely leave that to you.' Alice whimpered and Faith gathered her into her arms as she stood up, giving a careless little shrug as if it didn't matter. 'Tomorrow morning will do. Really.' What else could she say? 'If I wait until tomorrow I can go home through Melchester and pick up my wedding dress. It should be ready by then and it will save you the bother of sending it on.'

'It wouldn't have been any bother.' There was the faintest touch of irony in his voice, perhaps, as if he knew why she had mentioned it. She wished she was as certain.

But, once convinced that Faith wouldn't be leaving immediately, Alice went to bed like a lamb, suddenly exhausted by her long day and the excitement of her dress and the new kitten. She lay against the pillow, her cheeks pink with the reflected glow from the red pyjamas. She hadn't forgotten the bribe and clearly hadn't taken the least bit seriously Harry's warning that she wouldn't be having anything else for her birthday.

'Sarah's a pleasant girl,' Harry said as they made their way downstairs, leaving the new nanny to unpack and settle in. Peace having returned to his house, his temper was restored to its usual, slightly sardonic humour.

'Very pleasant.' She kept her hand closed about the frog in her pocket. Sarah had found it in her bath, obviously a present from Alice.

'Would you pop it somewhere safe in the garden?' she had asked, laughing as she handed it over without so much as a shudder. 'Cute little thing. I suppose Alice thought it would scare me, but I'd hate her to get into any more trouble with her uncle.'

'Unflappable,' Harry continued.

'I'd have to agree,' Faith said, trying hard not to squirm as the frog leapt within the cage of her hand. Sarah might think frogs were cute but they didn't have the same effect on her.

Harry gave her a long look. 'Remarkably level-headed, I thought.'

'Yes,' Faith agreed through clenched teeth.

'In fact I thought that since she is so capable we might leave her for a couple of hours this evening and go out to dinner. A small thank-you for helping.'

'Oh?' She was finding it increasingly hard to concentrate as the frog, after a moment's calm, began to flap inside her hand once more.

'Are you all right, Faith?'

'Fine,' she snapped. 'But I don't need thanking. And suppose Alice wakes up and thinks I've deserted her?'

'She'll understand if I explain that I want to thank you for staying . . . Are you sure you're all right, Faith? You look a little pale.' He took her elbow, dislodging her hand, and the frog, seizing the chance of freedom, leapt from her pocket, landing, a trifle dazed, at Harry's feet. 'Well, now.' He stooped and picked it up. 'Where did you come from?' He glanced at Faith. 'Sarah's bed?'

'Her bath.'

'And I wonder where Alice got the idea for that little stunt from?' Harry murmured.

'More to the point, where did she get the frog?' Faith gave a little shudder. 'Did you say something about dinner?'

'Twenty minutes?' He didn't betray his amusement by so much as the twitch of an eyelash. 'There's no need to dress up; it's not much more than a pub down by the river. But the food's good.'

She hadn't got anything fancy to wear, she thought as she surveyed her wardrobe a few minutes later. There was the skirt she had arrived in, the green trousers or her jeans. She'd worn her skirt all day and Ben had dribbled on her jeans. Not that she needed persuading to wear the green trousers. They had the kind of go-anywhere good looks that always made her feel special. She knew she looked good in them.

Does it matter? her subconscious demanded. And what about Julian? Her subconscious, she decided, had a point. A sensible, level-headed point. Then Faith rebelled against every sensible, rational, objective thought in her head. Besides, if she dressed as a dowd he would know why and he wouldn't hesitate to tell her so.

So she dressed with care, made an effort with her make-up and replaced the earrings that she had taken off the first painful time she discovered that babies liked to grab at them. But Harry made no comment as she came down the stairs. There was nothing in his face to show that he was impressed by her efforts. He probably wasn't, she thought a touch irritably as he ushered her into the dangerous wedge of black Porsche parked by the door.

'What a very . . . um . . . nice car,' Faith murmured as she settled in her seat, feeling the need to break the silence.

' 'Nice'? Just 'nice'?' His voice was ripe with mocking disbelief. 'I would have thought a girl who had the imagination to drive a *Spyder* could have come up with a more telling adjective than that. Or are you still trying to prove how *cool* you are?'

Faith refused to rise. She might be having an evening off from being level-headed. Stupid was something else. 'I did say *very* nice.'

'So you did.' He closed the door on her with the slightest smile and proceeded to take her breath away as they sped along a well-kept but deserted lane that led from the hall, climbing up through the trees until he turned into a yard surrounded on three sides by buildings that dated from the same period as the house. It didn't look like a pub of any kind, but before Faith could say so Harry turned to her with a questioning lift of his brows. 'Well, Miss Bridges, any advance on 'very nice'?'

'Should you be driving quite that fast along a country lane?' she replied primly.

'It's *my* country lane, Faith.' How easy it was to forget that Harry March lived off wealth accumulated by his more adventurous forebears, that he was a man who broke promises, that he was everything, in fact, that she most despised. When she didn't answer, he shrugged. 'At least you'll agree that it's an improvement on Lizzie's baby wagon.'

'The Range Rover is hers?'

'I don't have much use for baby seats,' he said wryly.

'No, I suppose not. But give it time. If getting your own way runs in the family you're far from safe.'

'Since you're the one with wedding bells ringing in her ears, I think it's safe to say that you'll be trading in your Alfa for a motorised pram long before I trade down to a family saloon.'

'Oh, the Alfa's doom is already written. I'll be putting it in the paper next week.'

'You're in such a hurry to start your family?'

'Not at all,' she replied, far too quickly. 'The world already has enough people, don't you think?' she added, in an effort to recover herself, but from Harry's shocked expression she realised she had not succeeded. 'But that's not the reason for the sale,' she rushed on, hoping he wouldn't say anything. 'It's really impossible to justify such a reckless waste of fuel to transport one person in this day and age. It doesn't even have a catalytic converter like the American version. I promised Julian . . .'

The frown creasing the space between dark brows deepened. 'What the hell are you talking about?' he demanded.

She bridled at his tone. 'In Julian's opinion we should all be using public transport — '

'Julian has a damned sight too many opinions. I shouldn't think there's much public transport in Antarctica.' She didn't bother to reply and he sat back, regarding her thoughtfully. 'But you're not going to live at the South Pole, are you, Faith? You've just been having a little joke at my expense.'

'When you thought you were the one doing all the teasing?'

'How wrong can you get?' He wasn't, apparently, amused.

She gave an awkward little shrug. 'Julian's been offered a post at Cambridge.'

'So, that's why you've left your job at the bank.'

'No, I could have transferred to another branch, but it would have meant giving up what I'm doing now. I'm going to

221

start my own consultancy.'

'Financial advice for environmentally concerned scientists? I'm sure Cambridge is overrun with them. But have they got any money to invest?'

'Don't mock it, Harry. We can't all be born with a silver spoon in our mouth or inherit a vast estate to keep us in luxury, but we're all looking for financial security. It's just that some of us are fussy about how the profits are made.'

'Well,' he said as he held the door for her, 'at least Cambridge is pretty flat. You'll be able to manage with a bike. You can always put a basket on the front for the shopping.'

She swung her legs out of the car and rose to her feet, refusing to be tormented for another moment. 'No basket,' she said. He hadn't stepped back as she'd unfolded herself from the car and now she was standing so close that she was assaulted by his own special scent overlaid with the cloth of his jacket — leather — a heady, intoxicating mixture that seemed to catch in her throat. Yet she mustn't step away, retreat, betray the power he possessed to weaken every resolve. Instead she lifted her chin, met his eyes head-on. 'If I'm going to ride a bicycle,' she declared, 'it'll be something sleek and fast with drop handlebars and . . . um . . . dozens of gears . . . ' She began to falter under his provoking gaze.

'In green, no doubt.'

'Green?' Stung, she retaliated, 'Not green, Harry. Red. Bright pillar-box red.'

Harry's mouth twisted into a smile that was pure mockery. 'East Anglian winters can be cold, you know. Nothing like the Antarctic, of course, but you'll freeze on a bike in that flimsy underwear. If you take my advice you'll swop your frills for something more substantial.'

'When I want your advice, Harry, I'll ask for it.' She turned away from the speculative look he was giving her.

'What is this place? It doesn't look like a pub.'

'It's not. This is my toy factory.'

She felt her jaw drop open. 'Toy factory?'

'I thought you might be interested.'

The door, painted black, looked conventional enough, except that there was no obvious way of opening it. 'It's voice-operated,' Harry explained. He took a small card from his pocket and handed it to her. 'This is the code. Why don't you try it?' Faith looked at him uncertainly. 'Just read it.'

She glanced at it. 'You're joking!'

'It's only a line of poetry, Faith. Chosen completely at random.'

She doubted that, but she gave a tiny shrug and began to quote stiffly from the card. ''Come live with me, and be my love. And we will all the pleasures prove . . . ''

'There now, that wasn't so hard, was it?'

'The door didn't open,' she pointed out.

'Perhaps if you invested your voice with a little warmth?' She glared at him. 'No? Of course, you're right. You could recite until Christmas and it wouldn't open for you.' Harry put the card in his pocket and, taking her hands in his, repeated the lines from Marlowe's poem with an intensity of feeling that made her blush. The door swung open.

She was impressed, but she wasn't about to show it. 'Very funny. Can we go now?'

'Don't you want to see the rest of my toys?'

'I would have thought a grown man had something better to do with his time.'

'It's a very profitable pastime. Surely, as a banker, that's of some interest to you?'

Her interest was aroused despite a feeling that it was a mistake to say so. 'Maybe. What kind of . . . ' she gave a little shrug to prove that she didn't care ' . . . toys do you make?'

'Well, not toys exactly. I design security systems.'

'Hence the fancy door?'

'It's just a bit of fun. I change the code to suit the client.'

She knew it. 'And is that all it is for you? A bit of fun?'

Suddenly he wasn't joking. 'No, Faith. I employ a team of highly skilled people to make and install my systems and I have a waiting list of clients happy to pay for the privilege. Wickham Hall may be a luxury, but it is an expensive one.'

'Why did you bring me here, Harry?' she demanded.

'Maybe I need a business loan.' She waited. 'Or maybe I just don't like being thought a layabout.'

'I don't believe you. You don't care tuppence what anyone thinks of you.'

'But you are not just anyone.' She refused to ask what he meant by that. He was flirting with her, tormenting a weakness that he had perceived in the carefully erected armour. It was all a game to him and he was clearly an expert. She flinched as he took her arm. He saw, but he had done with teasing. 'Come on, Faith,' he said abruptly. 'Let's go and have dinner.'

8

The restaurant was cool and inviting, with the river reflecting off the low, heavily beamed ceiling almost giving the impression of being on board a ship.

'This is lovely,' Faith said, looking around her once they had been settled at a quiet table by the window, determined to get the evening back on a less personal track. She sipped her drink. 'You must come here quite often; the staff seem to know you very well.' Polite, but formal. She was pleased with herself.

He gave her the benefit of a long, thoughtful look, but didn't confirm or deny it. 'The food's very good,' he said finally, as if that was explanation enough.

Faith studied the menu, satisfied that he had got the message. 'I wonder if the smoked trout will be as good as Mac's?'

'There's every chance. Why don't you ask him?'

She raised her eyes above the menu. 'Is he here?' Harry too had lifted his head, but he was looking at someone behind her. She turned to find Mac standing at her shoulder.

'You decided to stay at the hall after all?' he said, surprising her with the warmth of his smile, apparently genuinely pleased to see her.

'I had my arm twisted — '

'Not by me,' Harry murmured, and she favoured him with the briefest glare.

'But I'll be leaving tomorrow. Dinner is Harry's way of saying thank you . . . and goodbye.' She said the word with a finality that was unmistakable. 'Would you like to join us, Mac, or are you with someone?'

'Mac's presence is required in the kitchen,' Harry intervened smoothly. 'Faith wanted to know if the trout was as good as the one you brought up to the house the other night, Mac.'

'Oh, yes, I would say so. Why don't you try a little creamed horseradish with it?'

Faith glanced from one man to the other and the penny dropped. 'Oh, I see. *This* is Mac's place down by the river, right?'

'Right,' Harry confirmed.

'Thanks to the Major — '

'We're not in the army now, Mac. If you can't get used to Harry I'll start eating somewhere else.' He closed the menu. 'We'll both have the trout. And you can surprise us after that. You don't mind being surprised, do you, Faith?' His voice hinted at a challenge. She was more than up to it.

'If it's *Mac* doing the surprising, Harry, I look forward to it.'

'You'll not be disappointed.' The Scot grinned at Faith and she wondered why she had ever thought him dour. Maybe he'd just had enough of nappies and screaming babies on the first occasion they'd met. 'I'm glad you were able to stay for a while.'

'Why didn't you tell me?' Faith demanded the moment he had gone. 'You let me make an idiot of myself — all that talk about small business loans . . . '

'I didn't think you were an idiot and neither did Mac. You were very perceptive in fact. When I discovered how rocky the estate was after my father died he did suggest turning the place into an up-market hotel and restaurant . . . '

'But you couldn't do that.'

'I had to do something or put the place on the market. But I value my privacy, hence the 'toy' factory. It was touch-and-go for a while — but the threat of losing something precious concentrates the mind wonderfully. And it was all I had left.' He gave an awkward shrug, as if he had said too much. 'But I owed Mac something and this place was vacant . . . '

'So you offered it to him instead?'

'Little enough for saving my life.'

Faith wanted to ask the obvious question. It hung in the silence between them. 'I was dismantling a bomb. It went off.'

'A bomb?' She almost gagged on the word.

'That's what I did before I was obliged to retire from the army. Bomb disposal. In this case it was something uncovered by construction workers at a disused military base.' He continued, his voice quite without expression. 'It was one of ours, which should have made it simple — '

'Bomb disposal?' The very idea made her feel sick.

'Just the job for a reckless little boy prone to climbing out of bedroom windows, don't you think?'

'It . . . it doesn't seem to have been a long-term career move. What happened?'

'Oh, the bomb was donkey's years old. It was a miracle it didn't go off when it was unearthed and take half a dozen construction workers with it.' He paused. 'You're looking a little pale, Faith. Shall we skip the gory details?'

She didn't need the gory details. She'd seen the result. 'I'm fine,' she lied. 'I . . . I've seen far worse injuries at the swimming club.'

'In other words I really shouldn't feel sorry for myself?' There was an ironic challenge behind the words that made her bristle.

'No, Harry. After all, you've got more than most people could ever dream of. Even your business is a hobby.'

'A hobby that pays the wages of a dozen people and keeps the roof over my head. But you're right about the bomb. I was careless . . . I'm just glad that no one else was injured. However, I lost the two things that meant most to me at the time — my job and the girl I was going to marry.'

Clementine? Clementine had dumped him? Surely not . . . Confused, she said, 'You could have lost your life.'

'And one must be grateful?'

'There are other jobs. And other

girls. You only have one life.'

'You are a pragmatist, Miss Bridges.'

'And it takes a romantic to be a hero?'

'A hero?' A small sound signalled his disgust with the word. 'An idiot. My only excuse is that I was getting married that weekend and I had my mind on . . . well, other things.' His mouth tightened in a self-deprecating little smile.

His bride-to-be. What man in his right mind wouldn't have been thinking about her? Conscious that she had forced something into the open that he would rather not discuss, she made an effort to turn the conversation from the girl he had planned to marry.

'I knew you were in the army, of course,' she said, hoping to divert him. 'Janet has a photograph of you in your uniform — '

'In a silver frame. I know. My mother gave it to her. It was cheaper than a pension,' he said bitterly.

'But she has a pension . . . Oh, I see. That was from you.' He neither confirmed nor denied it and Faith was aware of a dark mood settling over him. Guilt poked hard at her conscience. She had accused him openly of idleness and she had been wrong. Far worse, deep inside herself she had tried him and found him guilty of walking out on a girl who'd loved him, but she had been wrong about that too. She didn't know what had happened, but it was obviously nothing so simple.

They said that confession was good for the soul. She would try it. Maybe it would help. 'I thought you'd jilted Clementine,' she said.

'I noticed. Why does it bother you so much?'

'I suppose . . . I suppose because it happened to me.' He looked up sharply. 'At the same time. Aunt Janet was planning to wear the same grand outfit to both our weddings.'

'Oh, I see.' He let out a long breath, as if he had been holding it for ever. 'You must have been very young. What happened?'

'Oh, nothing dramatic.' She braved a smile. 'No row; there wasn't another girl; he just got cold feet. He went to Canada two days before the wedding.'

'Canada?'

'The Foreign Legion wouldn't have occurred to him. He didn't have that much imagination.' That was supposed to make him laugh, but he didn't. 'He has a software business there now.' As well as a wife and two children. It wasn't marriage he had run from, just her.

'Is that why you're marrying Julian Fellowes even though you don't love him?'

Was it? Did it matter? She refused to think about it, laughed the idea away. 'Oh, Harry, I've been in love dozens of times since then. Hundreds of times . . .'

He didn't respond to her brittle attempt at gaiety but regarded her intently. 'I haven't known you long, Faith, but I find that a little difficult to believe.'

She dropped her eyes to the tablecloth. 'Well, perhaps I was overstating my case . . . just a little.'

'Just a little? I've only managed it the

once myself.' He stretched across the table, lifted her chin so that she had no choice but meet his eyes. 'I'd consider it a kindness if you could show me how it's done.'

The touch of his fingers was sending tremors through her. She wanted to show him — take him in her arms and tell him that love wasn't something you could learn. It was something rare and wonderful that just happened. Out of the blue. 'You broke off the engagement for her, didn't you?' She felt her voice tremble. 'Let her go?'

He dropped his hand. 'Well, I couldn't saddle the poor girl with a wreck — '

'But you're not — '

'No?' He was holding onto his feelings, but his eyes were shadowed. 'Well, perhaps not as much as everyone was convinced I was going to be. But Clemmie was built for fun. She took one look at me lying in my hospital bed and had hysterics.'

'I don't think she would now.'

'No?' He shrugged. 'Maybe not. But I'm not the Harry March in Janet's photograph, am I? Not the life-and-soul-of-the-party Harry March. Not the Harry March that made other girls envious of Clemmie. Not the same man at all.'

No. Older, wiser. Infinitely more desirable. 'You make her sound very shallow. She might have been attracted by the way you looked, but it takes more than that to fall in love.'

'Maybe. But the thing I kept asking myself was how I would have felt if the situation had been reversed. If she had been lying in a hospital bed with her face in ruins and the very real possibility that she might lose a leg.' He wasn't looking at her but into the glass he was holding, staring into the bottom of it as if it might be able to offer him the answers he sought.

'Did you come up with an answer?'

He refused to meet her eyes. 'Only that I wasn't going to inflict that on her.'

'You didn't give her a chance — '

'To prove how noble she was?' His mouth tightened. 'Would you want someone to marry you because it was the noble thing to do? How long do you think it would have lasted before one of us had ended up hating the other . . . ?' He lifted his shoulders — not quite a shrug. 'The wedding had to be cancelled anyway, so I suggested she take one of her friends to Bermuda, have some fun . . . '

'Bermuda? Why Bermuda?'

He looked up. 'Oh, we were going there for our honeymoon. A friend had loaned us the villa. It seemed a shame to waste the tickets.'

He hadn't heard of travel insurance? Or was she being too practical, too level-headed? 'Surely she didn't go?' No girl could bear to walk away from the man she was supposed to love and use the honeymoon they had planned as an . . . escape? Could she? She saw from his face that Clemmie Norwood could, and had.

'It was only when she had gone that I realised how much I wanted her to tell me not to be so stupid, that we'd get married in the hospital chapel right away and nothing would matter except being together. The fact that she went at all told me everything I needed to know; I didn't wait for her to give me back my ring. Pride'll get you through all kinds of pain, Faith.'

'That's what Janet meant?'

'That and more. In the end it was pride that made me cling to a shattered leg when consultants and common sense suggested otherwise. I had this idea in my head, you see, that one day, at a party, I would walk up to her and quite casually ask her to dance. And afterwards simply walk away. Just to let her know that she'd been wrong . . . '

'And did you?'

'Well, the walking bit took longer than I thought.' He managed a wry smile. 'By the time I was sufficiently mobile to dance she was married to someone else and too advanced in pregnancy to tango.'

'Well, I hope her ankles were swollen.'

'What?' Then he realised what she had said and quite suddenly he laughed. 'I doubt it. Clemmie would never have been seen in public with swollen ankles.'

Faith thought that Miss Clementine Norwood sounded a complete beast, but she kept that thought to herself. The food arrived and Harry deliberately changed the topic of conversation.

'Tell me your plans for this consultancy of yours, Faith.'

She looked at him uncertainly, but it was a neutral subject and for the rest of the meal, under his careful questioning, she began enthusiastically to expound her ideas. 'The returns are not always quite as high, but as more and more people are becoming interested in the idea, voting with their money, more companies are making an effort to meet the criteria.'

'I admire your commitment.'

'That's what Julian said.'

'Did he? I must be losing my touch; I used to be considered quite original.' He tucked his hand beneath her elbow as they left the restaurant.

'He *meant* it, Harry.'

'So did I. But then I suppose his role as a caring environmentalist put his sincerity on an altogether higher plane than mine.' He looked up at the sky, the grey silk bubbles of cloud still faintly charged with pink from the dying sun. 'It's a lovely evening; shall we walk back? It's only half a mile.'

'I'd like that. Very environmentally friendly.' She couldn't resist teasing him just a little.

'I'm getting the idea. You'll be converting me to low-energy light bulbs next.'

'You should seriously consider it. Save money and the earth at the same time. Will your car be safe in the car park?'

'The car will be fine. I often walk back after a meal. Mac has a key and he'll lock it up in his garage when he closes up.'

They walked in silence for a while, enjoying the secretive sounds of small animals in the undergrowth, startling a late rabbit, breathing in the night scent of wild honeysuckle.

'I can understand why you wanted to keep the manor,' Faith said finally. 'If this was my home I wouldn't give it up without a fight either.'

Harry paused, turned to her. His arm was along her shoulder; she didn't remember his putting it there, but it had seemed quite natural, quite right to rest her head against the warmth of his shoulder. 'Then stay, Faith. For as long as you like.'

'Stay . . . ?' But he had a nanny for Ben and Alice. 'What do you mean?'

'This.' He drew her against him, tilting her head back over his arm, and kissed her. Her lips parted without coaxing and he took possession of her mouth, plundering it as a man wandering lost in a desert would have fallen

243

upon water. It was thrilling, glorious to be kissed with such determination under the summer stars, and for a moment she surrendered herself, willingly, joyfully. It was part of the magic of the night, the moment. Tomorrow it would be over. She would be gone. Life would be back to normal. But for now . . .

For now her breasts were peaking with the frantic desire that surged through her like an express train and her arms slid around Harry's neck as she swayed against him, her legs almost buckling beneath her. He caught her round the waist and held her close so that she could feel the urgency of his own need, breathe in the musky male scent of him until it filled her head, her throat, her entire being.

'I want you, Faith,' he murmured.

She wanted him too. She would marry Julian because she had given her word, because it was the sane, sensible thing to do, but Harry March would always be the dream lover who came to her in the darkness of the night to fire her dreams . . . A stab of headlights in the dark lit up the lane, and the moment and the thought were drowned out by the throaty roar of a powerful engine.

'Harry?' It was Mac. He climbed from the Porsche, leaving the engine running. 'Alice isn't well. Your nanny just called. She's already sent for the doctor but I thought you'd want your car — '

'Get in.' Harry barked the words at Faith and before she had even fastened her seat belt the car was rocketing up the road, leaving Mac standing where, a moment before, they had been locked in a passionate embrace. A long shudder swept through her at the thought of what she had so nearly done. Another moment and they would have been lying on the grass tearing at one another's clothes. Harry, however, had other things on his mind now. He slewed the car to a halt in front of the house and ran up the steps, leaving her to follow.

'Sarah!' He didn't wait for an answer

but bounded up the stairs two at a time. Just as he reached the top step Alice's kitten stepped off the edge of the carpet and skittered with a startled mew across the polished wood of the floor. Faith's shout of warning came too late as Harry, twisting awkwardly to avoid putting his foot on the little scrap of fur, fell, his leg giving way beneath him and sending him sprawling on the floor.

'Damn! Damn! Damn!' Harry swore with quiet vehemence as his face contorted with pain. 'I thought I said that animal wasn't allowed upstairs!'

'Can I help?' But Faith's tentative offer was brushed aside as he dragged himself to his feet and limped heavily towards the nursery.

'What's the matter with her?' he asked urgently, the greyness of his face having more to do with concern for Alice than his own pain.

The little girl was lying on her bed, limp and damp with sweat, looking half her normal size. Sarah, applying a cold cloth to her forehead and cheeks, turned away long enough to say, 'She's got a temperature and her glands are swollen. It came on so suddenly . . . It might just be a cold, but it's so hard to tell with children, especially when you don't know them. I've sent for the doctor.'

A distant peal on the bell announced his arrival. 'I'll let him in,' Faith said, feeling utterly helpless and glad of something useful to do. She ran back down the stairs, explaining the situation to the doctor as she took him up to the nursery. He didn't stay long.

'Just treat the fever as you have been doing. I don't think it's more than a cold. Elizabeth used to get just the same way. I'll drop in again before surgery in the morning and I'm sure I'll see an improvement, but if there's any change for the worse call me straight away.'

Harry's limp, more noticeable since his tumble, caught the doctor's eye. 'What have you been doing to yourself?' the older man asked as they went down the stairs. Faith didn't hear his reply.

'Faith?' Sarah touched her arm to attract her attention and she tore her eyes away from Harry.

'Sorry. What did you say?'

'Alice is asking for her mother. Could you stay with her while I move Ben into my room? It's probably too late to stop him catching whatever ails Alice, but it's worth a try.'

'Um . . . yes.' She pulled herself together. 'Yes, of course. You take care of Ben; I'll see to Alice.'

'She'll probably respond better to you . . . If you can persuade her to take a drink . . . '

Faith sat down on the edge of the child's bed and began to bathe her face with the cool flannel.

'Faith?'

'Yes, darling?'

'You won't leave me, will you? You won't go away,' Alice begged pitifully. Her eyes suddenly filled with tears. 'Stay till my mummy comes home. Please.'

Faith's heart went out to the child and she leaned over and kissed her forehead. 'I won't go anywhere, sweetheart. I'll be here as long as you need me.'

'You promise?'

She didn't hesitate. 'I promise,' she said. 'But you'll have to do something for me.'

'What is it?'

'I want you to try and have a drink.' She lifted a glass of barley water to the little girl's lips. 'It will help to cool you down.'

Faith waited patiently while Alice took a few sips, then she settled her down against the pillow. After that the child seemed to drift off into a restless sleep and Faith pulled a chair nearer to the bed and sat down, holding Alice's hand lightly in her own, her mind drifting back to her own childhood illnesses and the way her mother had always been there when she'd woken. She knew how much Alice was missing her mother. No one better.

'How is she?' Harry came alongside

her and stood there staring down at his niece.

'She'll be fine.' Faith, too, kept her eyes on Alice. She had managed, until now, to block out the scene that Mac had interrupted. She wanted to keep it that way. 'How are you?'

'Me?'

'Did the doctor look at your leg?'

'There isn't any point. I don't fall over quite as much as I used to, but sometimes I forget that I can't run any more . . . '

'You nearly tripped over a cat. It could have happened to anyone.'

'Could it?' he said, just a touch too sharply, looking around. 'Where did the little wretch go?'

'He ran for his life. He'll come back when he thinks the coast is clear. Look, why don't you go and lie down? You can't do anything here.'

He shook his head. 'I can't leave her.'

She could understand his feelings, but he couldn't just stand there all night. 'Well, if you insist on staying, go and lie down over there.' She indicated a bed that was the twin of Alice's. 'After all, you won't be any use to man or beast if your leg is too painful to walk on tomorrow.'

For the first time since their mad dash back to the manor, Harry's face relaxed into something that might just have been interpreted as a smile. 'Did anyone ever tell you that you've got a distinctly bossy streak? Just like your aunt.'

'In that case you'll know there's absolutely no point in arguing with me.'

'No, ma'am.'

'And don't make fun of me either,' she said, turning to look up at him.

'I wouldn't dream of it.' He bent and dropped a kiss on her upturned face. 'I'm glad you're staying.'

'Staying?'

'I heard you promise Alice that you would.'

'That's right. I promised Alice.' She might have lost her head temporarily, but she wasn't crazy. He had obviously never got over Clemmie Norwood's betrayal and she was marrying Julian in three weeks' time. The days were ticking by with remorseless determination. 'It has nothing to do with you.'

He straightened abruptly. 'Did I suggest it was?' He didn't wait for an answer but limped heavily across the room to the spare bed and, after removing his shoes, lowered himself onto it and lay there, stiff and still.

'Harry?'

'What is it?' His voice was discouraging.

'I wondered . . . ' He turned fierce blue eyes on her and she almost lost her nerve. 'Would it help if I . . . ' she swallowed ' . . . well, if I were to massage your leg . . . ?'

'Is there no end to your talents, Faith? Or are you determined to extract every ounce of retribution for your enforced stay?'

'Retribution?'

'Do you want me to spell it out for you?'

Faith swallowed, too mortified by what he was thinking to blush. 'I wasn't . . . I didn't . . . '

He must have seen her flinch because his voice softened a little. 'Didn't you?'

'The physio . . . at the swimming club . . . She showed me when Dad had problems with his calves . . . all that standing about in cold churches . . . ' Under his fierce gaze the words came out in jerky, disjointed little rushes, like a clockwork doll winding down.

'Well, thanks for the offer, Faith,' he said, when he was sure she had stopped. 'But if you don't mind I'll take a raincheck.'

Alice stirred restlessly and Faith turned thankfully to the child. By the time she had sponged her face and persuaded her to have another drink, Sarah was at her side with two cups of tea. 'Can I do anything?' she whispered.

'No. I'll stay here. I'd be happier if you were the one keeping an eye on Ben. Is he all right?'

'Fine so far. Give me shout if you

want a break.' Sarah nodded towards Harry. 'He obviously doesn't want this cup of tea. I might as well have it.' She tiptoed from the room, taking it with her.

Harry had apparently dropped off to sleep and Faith found herself stupidly near the brink of tears as she saw that Alice's kitten had crept up onto the bed and was fast asleep at his feet.

It was still and silent in the room and Faith sat back in the chair and tried to sort out her thoughts. About Harry. About Julian. Julian, who was coming home in a couple of weeks' time to marry her. But would it be right, when there was no use in denying that she was so physically attracted to another man?

Or was it just that being thrown into such close contact with Harry had stirred up an emotional stew that had been simmering quietly for years beneath that controlled surface the world saw?

Her eyes were drawn to his sleeping figure, to the dark head on the pillow, the thick mop of hair that tangled with the crumpled collar of his chambray shirt. He might have lost his head-turning looks. He was irritable, tormenting, more nightmare than dream. Yet he inflamed her, excited her, made her feel utterly foolish. She should have hated it, but she didn't. And that made her wonder about Harry's much vaunted white heat of passion. For the first time since Michael had broken her young heart, she wondered if it was, after all, worth a second risk . . .

Faith's head fell forward, jerking her awake with a sickening wrench. She looked around, gathering her woolly thoughts as she glanced at her watch. It was nearly four o'clock.

She stood up, laid her hand lightly on Alice's forehead. She was cooler, sleeping more easily now, and Faith stretched, trying to get some life back into her stiff limbs. Harry, his back turned towards her, the kitten nestled behind his knees, was lying still except for the slow rise and fall of his chest and she envied him the comfort of the bed. But, tempting as it was to go and lie down, she was afraid that Alice might wake up and miss her . . .

She glanced again at Harry, wishing she hadn't been so quick to suggest he lie down and rest his leg. She sat down, tried to get comfortable, but the chair felt like concrete, and as she stood up again and paced the floor in an effort to ease her aching limbs the bed seemed to beckon invitingly. It was a single bed but a large one, and with Harry lying on his side there was plenty of room for two. And he was fast asleep . . . He would never know that she rested there just for a moment . . .

Faith lowered herself beside him, easing her feet off the floor, and very gently lay back against the pillow. It was bliss. The kitten yawned, stretched, his claws extended, and Faith scooped him up and put him on her stomach before he sank them into Harry's leg. She'd go downstairs in a moment, make a cup of tea, take him with her. The kitten purred like a tiny dynamo as he trod against her for a moment before curling up contentedly. She closed her eyes. Just for a moment. Just to shut out the night-light.

When she opened them again she blinked and groaned. 'Turn off the light,' she mumbled into the pillow.

'It's not the light. It's the sun,' Alice whispered.

She opened her eyes again and screwed them up against the fierce light. The sun had crept above the sill of the tall sash-window and was shining directly into her eyes. Alice smiled sleepily at her from the other bed, all the dangerous night flush gone.

'Hello, Alice,' she said, making a determined effort to rouse herself but not succeeding.

'You stayed,' Alice whispered. 'All night.'

'I promised. How are you feeling?'

'Like a frog. All croaky.'

'I think the less said about frogs the better, don't you?' Faith replied, a little croaky herself with sheer relief. 'Would you like some juice?' She made a move to swing off the bed but found that she couldn't.

'I'm dry too. Will you get some for me?' Harry's voice in her ear jerked her into full consciousness, even as his arm about her waist tightened to hold her captive. She half turned, a protest on her lips, but the words caught in her throat. He looked so thoroughly endearing, his hair tousled, his chin shadowed with morning bristles. Then he grinned and she blushed scarlet as the full impact of the situation was borne in upon her.

9

Faith swallowed. It was important, desperately important, to appear unconcerned in the face of mind-numbing embarrassment. A slight smile should do it. Very slight and very cool. The kind she employed to put amorous investment analysts in their place. It had never failed her in the past. But Harry's arm was tight around her waist and she could feel the heat of his body, the power-packed curve of his chest, abdomen, thighs from her shoulder to her foot, which she realised was nestling cosily against his ankle as if that were precisely where it was meant to be . . . Cool flew out of the window. 'I — I only meant to close my eyes for a moment . . . ' she found herself stammering.

'You have an open invitation to close your eyes in my bed any time, Miss Bridges. You don't snore. You don't kick. In fact I only have one complaint.'

'Complaint?' What on earth had he to complain about?

'I don't like your nightwear. Next time I'd prefer the red silk — '

'Next time?' Fury finally loosened her tongue. 'There isn't going to be any — '

'Well, don't you two look cosy?' Sarah said, appearing in the doorway and defusing the imminent explosion. 'Like a pair of teaspoons in a drawer. How's the invalid?'

'Decidedly brighter,' Harry said, ignoring Faith's furious attempts to disentangle herself from his grasp beneath the bedcover. Cover? He had woken up and covered them both and then . . . and then . . . got back in beside her? She groaned — a small desperate sound, imperceptible to anyone who wasn't pressed up close. 'But she's thirsty,' Harry continued, with the faintest suggestion of a chuckle in his voice.

'I'll get her some juice,' Faith said, making a determined bid for freedom.

'I've brought some,' Sarah said, no help at all.

'Well, I'll take Tiddles downstairs. He shouldn't be in the bedroom. I was going to do it last night . . . I didn't mean to go to sleep. I can't think . . . ' She wished that weren't true. She was thinking far too clearly. So was Sarah. And it was quite clear what Sarah was thinking . . .

'Hush, Faith,' Harry murmured, close to her ear, as if he had a direct line to her thoughts and was enjoying them enormously. 'You're only making things worse.'

'But it's true . . . ' she protested, apparently quite unable to stop. 'Aunt Janet would never allow it — '

'You sound more like her with every passing day. What a shame you won't be putting all this experience to good use.'

That was when she stopped worrying about what Sarah might be *thinking* and began to worry about what her aunt had been *saying*. 'What?' she demanded, quite forgetting that they had an audience. 'What has Aunt Janet been telling you?'

'What is there to tell?' Harry's look was thoughtful as he dropped a kiss on her tousled head then released her, rolling away to sit on the far side of the bed, raking his long fingers through his hair. 'How's Ben?' he asked Sarah, apparently not in the least put out to be discovered in a single bed with a girl who was about to marry someone else.

'Fine. No symptoms. Yet.' Sarah ran a professional hand over Alice's forehead. Alice scowled and pulled away. 'And this one's a lot cooler.'

He rose to his feet, still favouring his good leg, and retrieved the mewing scrap of fluff from the bed. 'Well, the doc can look at them both later.' He regarded the wriggling cat with amusement. 'Come on, Tiddles. She who must be obeyed has spoken. Downstairs where you belong.' His departure left a sudden vacuum. An unbearable silence.

'He just . . . I just . . . ' Faith rushed in, feeling somehow that she should offer Sarah an explanation. The words wouldn't come and she wondered bleakly what had happened to the self-confident woman with her life under perfect control who had arrived at Wickham Ash . . . was it really only three days ago? 'Well, anyway,' she said, in a desperate little rush, 'it wasn't what you think.'

'Oh, I make it a rule never to think before six-thirty,' Sarah said solemnly. 'Or before I've had a cup of tea. Whichever is later. Can I make one for you?'

Grateful for her tact, Faith responded with a somewhat rueful grin. 'I'm beginning to think that I'm beyond help. But a cup of tea would be lovely.' She eased herself to her feet. 'Then I'd better have a shower.' A cold, fierce blast of reality might concentrate her wits.

'Well, take your time; have a nap if you want. You couldn't have had much sleep last night.' She seemed quite unaware of Faith's sudden tremor, or that her words had a double edge.

'Rather too much, under the circumstances. I didn't mean to go to sleep at all.'

'Well, the crisis seems to be over.'

'Does it?' Faith would have given a great deal to be sure of that.

'For the moment. With children you can never tell.' As Sarah turned to go, she stopped in the doorway. 'Oh, by the way, your father rang last night while you were out. I'm sorry, but with all the drama it went right out of my mind.'

'Did he sound concerned? My aunt's in hospital . . . '

Faith immediately dismissed her own troubles from her mind, but Sarah was reassuring. 'He said not to worry. In fact, he seemed very glad that you'd gone out for the evening. He said it would do you good.'

Which just went to show how much he knew. 'Oh, well,' she said, glancing at her watch, 'I suppose it is a bit early to ring him.'

'I'm sure it'll wait until you've had

your shower and some breakfast. There's nothing worse than sleeping in your clothes, is there?' Sarah said as she wandered off, yawning, to make the tea.

Isn't there? Faith headed for her own room and the needle-sharp chill of the shower. She had her doubts about that. On this occasion she would have rated sleeping *without* them an absolute disaster.

★ ★ ★

Faith returned her father's call as soon as she had coaxed Alice to eat a little yogurt for her breakfast, but all she got was the answering machine. She called her aunt, hoping to find him at the hospital, but Janet Bridges hadn't seen her brother and was far more interested in the health of little Alice.

'Make sure she has plenty of fluids and don't let her get too excited. Elizabeth could never handle excitement. It used to bring her out in a rash. Or was that Emerald Fitzsimmon? Oh,

Faith, I'm getting old.'

'Don't be silly. You've just had major surgery. Once you're back on your feet there'll be no holding you.'

'It'll be a week or two yet,' she grumbled.

'I want you at my wedding. In a wheelchair if necessary. You can decorate it with white bows — '

'Humph. We'll see about that. How's Harry?'

'Harry is . . . What Harry is isn't repeatable,' she said, with feeling.

'He's getting to you, is he?' Janet Bridges chuckled.

'Was that the plan?'

'Plan? I don't know what you mean.' Her indignation was utterly convincing. It wasn't until Faith had hung up that she realised her aunt hadn't asked her why she was still in Wickham Ash.

The jangle of the doorbell distracted her.

★ ★ ★

After the doctor had left, uttering soothing assurances to Harry that Alice's glands would reduce in size in their own good time and that he was almost certain that it wasn't mumps but he'd call in again and check on her progress, she knew there had been something bothering her but couldn't remember what.

'Penny for your thoughts?'

Faith looked up as Harry returned from seeing the doctor to his car. 'They're not worth as much as that. My head's stuffed with cotton wool.'

'A swim would clear your head. Sarah can hold the fort upstairs for half an hour.'

'I have the feeling that Sarah could man the battlements of the Tower of London single-handed,' she said, but was unwilling to risk the kind of close encounter that swimming represented.

'It's a shame that Alice doesn't like her.'

'I can't think why, but you don't have to turn the screw, Harry; I'm not about to desert her. I feel bad enough that I was out enjoying myself when she was sick — '

'You are prepared to admit you were enjoying yourself?'

'Of course I enjoyed myself. I'm sorry that I didn't have the opportunity to thank you properly last night.'

'You were getting there, but since you're staying you'll have plenty of time to get round to it.'

She felt her cheeks sting with colour but made a heroic effort to ignore the fact. 'I've promised Alice I'll stay until her mother returns. Heaven knows how I'm going to organise my wedding at long distance, but, with Sarah looking after Ben, I'll try. You've got what you wanted, Harry, so can we leave it at that?'

'If you think that's what I wanted, Faith, I'm happy to disabuse you any time. But perhaps now would be a good time to tell you that your wedding invitations will be arriving by courier this morning.'

'They're coming here? You went ahead and arranged that without consulting me?'

'I was trying to be helpful. Of course if you've changed your mind — '

'About staying?'

'About the wedding, Faith,' he said, quite gently. 'There's no compulsion to get married, you know. People *don't* get married all the time and survive to tell the tale. *I know.*'

But they didn't survive unscathed. 'Of course I haven't changed my mind,' she said, with a determination that rang hollow in her own ears. 'What ever gave you that idea?'

He reached out and touched her lips, his eyes lit with a provoking little smile. 'I can't imagine.'

'Harry! Please!' she begged as a shiver ran through her and, terrified of her own weakness, she turned away from him.

'Please what, Faith?' he asked. His hands were resting so lightly on her shoulders, his breath so soft against her hair that

269

she might have been imagining it. Except that her heart was pumping with excitement, her very skin rippling beneath his touch.

'Please . . . don't,' she begged.

'Don't?' His hands tightened. 'Look at yourself in the mirror, Faith. There, see?' She opened her eyes unwillingly, closed them again as she was confronted by her reflection in the mirror that hung above the fireplace. Her cheeks were hectically flushed, her breasts rising and falling too quickly; Harry's face above hers, the pair of them were framed like a photograph by the ornate gilt frame. 'You do see, don't you, Faith? Your head is saying one thing, but the rest of you is saying something quite different.'

She couldn't deny it, but she didn't have to succumb to the temptation. 'It's got nothing to do with love,' she said, turning away from the disturbing image in the mirror.

'What is love? Is it something that can be written down on paper and sent through the post? Pretty words that — '

'Julian cares about things,' she blurted out — anything to stop the dangerous words that seemed to threaten everything she stood for, wanted. 'Important things.' She turned to face him.

'Unlike me?'

'You don't understand, Harry . . . '

'I understand that love at long distance is very safe. You can detach yourself from emotion, analyse your feelings like a set of accounts. It's what you're best at, isn't it, Faith? That's why you're so good at your job. That's why you can contemplate marrying a man you scarcely know.'

'Is knowing a man any guarantee of happiness? I'd known Michael all my life. I thought I knew him better than anyone but he still hurt me . . . '

'First love seems very real, but it's just nature's way of shaking out the emotions, giving them a trial run. We need to mature a little before we're ready to commit ourselves for life.'

'Yes, well, I'm all grown up now — '

'Are you? I think perhaps you're still eighteen, emotionally.'

'And you'd like to help me grow up a little?' Her challenge was direct and he met it without flinching.

'Any time you like. And then if you still want to marry Julian . . . ' He gave the smallest shrug.

'You conceited — ' She swung at him, but he caught her wrist and held her.

'What ever happened to the level-headed Miss Faith Bridges?' he enquired, a tormenting grin lighting his eyes.

'You could agitate a statue!' she declared, trying to pull free. He merely took the opportunity to capture her free hand.

'Thank you.'

'That wasn't a compliment!' She stood, her breasts heaving with indignation. 'You just don't understand. Julian and I — ' She stopped, unwilling to expose herself further to Harry's ridicule.

'You and Julian . . . ?' he prompted.

'It isn't like that! It's not simply lust — '

'After a long spell in the icy wastes Julian might not feel quite the same. You'd better prepare yourself.'

'Harry . . . ' Her protest died on her lips as, still holding her wrists, he drew her closer to him.

'For instance, what would you do if he were here in this room right now, holding you in his arms? How would you feel?' She didn't know how she would feel; she only knew how Harry made her feel — breathless with anticipation, light-headed, unable to move as he took her hands and raised them to his lips, kissing the tips of her fingers one by one without ever taking his eyes from hers. 'That's fairly innocent. Could you handle that?'

Innocent? It didn't feel innocent. It felt dangerously exciting, churning up the kind of feelings that were anything but innocent. She tried very hard to concentrate on Julian, but every touch of Harry's lips sent a little charge through her, so that her breath rose higher in her throat and she was unable to answer, unable to think of anything outside the small circle formed by their bodies. He turned her hands over and his lips brushed her palms. She visibly trembled. 'That seems to be a little bit more of a problem.'

'I . . . ' Her throat clammed up. He released her hands and she almost shook with what she hoped was relief as he straightened. Too soon. There was no relief as he cradled her face between long, sensitive hands. There would never be any relief until she found the strength to tear herself away from Harry's drugging touch. She must stop him. Right now. All she had to do was walk away. But her legs, like her voice, didn't seem to be working.

'Did he ever kiss you, Faith? Or were you too busy discussing how you were going to save the world? Perhaps a marriage of minds doesn't need passion. And since you've apparently decided not to have any children I

suppose you won't actually need sex
. . . Or are you having second thoughts
about that?'

'No!'

'I've seen you with Ben in the middle
of the night, half-asleep, your hair
tumbled about your shoulders, eyes full
of love. You looked so warm, so beautiful, Faith. I wanted you so much . . . '

'Harry, please.' She mouthed the
words; no sound came out.

' 'Let me not to the marriage of true
minds/Admit impediments . . . ' Tell
me, does this true-minded man know
that you blush like a peach ripening on
a sunny wall, Faith? Or how your skin
feels beneath his hands? Does he care?'
He stroked her temple lightly with the
pad of his thumb. 'It's like translucent
silk; I can see the faint violet-blue
tracery of your veins . . . ' She felt her
pulse throbbing beneath his touch,
warm and vital. 'Does he know that
your hair smells of apple blossom?'
Somehow her cheek was resting against
the softness of his shirt while his

275

fingers, his face were buried in her hair.

'It's just . . . ' Shampoo. She must be going mad, she thought. She should be telling him to stop, but she was mesmerised by the touch of his hands, the soft, lulling drawl of his voice.

He lifted her face, tilting it up so that his own was just above her, too close. Not close enough. 'Does he know that when you part your lips, just a little, so that your teeth show, you look like a kitten asking to be stroked?' He clearly didn't expect an answer because he brushed his mouth against hers, stroking her . . . and suddenly she knew why cats purred.

Her mind was clamouring a warning — a flashing-red-light, wailing Klaxon kind of warning — but her body wasn't listening. Her lips were throbbing, demanding the kiss that hovered, and then her body was drowning in the sweetness of it as he took her lower lip between his lips and stroked it with the tip of his tongue. There was no thought of danger as he drew her close, one hand tangled in her hair, one at her waist, holding her to him so that she could feel his need for her. This was it. Passion. White-hot. No holds barred, no prisoners taken. She wanted Harry, and in that moment nothing mattered more than that she show him how much.

It seemed for ever before they finally parted, a lifetime of bliss before he raised his head and she saw the flash of something like triumph in his eyes. 'Tell me, Faith,' he asked softly. 'Was that better than a cross on the bottom of a letter?'

And that finally released her from the madness that had seized her. She wanted to hit him, slap that look of triumph from his face, wipe out his memory of how her mouth had felt, had tasted. But she didn't because she knew he was right. He had seen her desire and reacted to it. She had not been an unwilling partner to his love-making. But for her it had been real. Real feelings, real emotions. He had been doing nothing more than proving a point.

Well, he had proved it. Did he expect

her to fall into his bed — a temporary lover as well as temporary nanny? In the white heat of passion she might have succumbed to temptation, but, knowing that he was simply providing a tutorial for a girl he thought emotionally immature, in need of warming up . . . Even so, it took all her strength to step back from the brink.

'When I've tried the cross in person,' she said, with admirable restraint, 'I'll let you know.'

'You'll what?' Disbelief flashed across his face, followed closely by something bordering on disgust. 'You're not being honest with yourself, Faith. Worse, you're not being honest with a man who wants to marry you. He can't be that much of a cold fish — '

'I made a promise.'

'Promises and pie-crusts are made to be broken,' he retorted.

'Are they?' She made her voice hard. 'I thought you might understand the importance of a promise better than most, Harry.'

'Did you?' His eyes darkened. 'Then I'm sorry to disappoint you. Clemmie might have been vain and facile, the kind of girl who never gave a promise a second thought if it suited her, but she knew what she wanted out of life and went for it. It gave her a basic kind of honesty. You should try it some time.'

'I know what I want,' she said stiffly.

'Really?' His eyes clouded with anger. 'Then last night was a figment of my imagination? And five minutes ago that was some other girl kissing me as if her life depended on it?' He didn't wait for her answer, but turned abruptly and walked from the room.

★ ★ ★

'Didn't anyone hear the bell?' Sarah startled her. She had no idea how long she had been standing in the drawing room staring at nothing while her mind tried to reel back into place the emotions that Harry had unravelled.

279

But she couldn't even find the end to make a start.

'What? Oh, Sarah, I'm sorry. I was miles away.'

'Well, hurry back, girl. Your wedding dress has just been delivered and I, for one, can't wait to see it.'

'My wedding dress?' What grotesque irony had brought it to the door just at that moment?

'The young woman who delivered it asked if you would try it on to check the length as soon as possible,' Sarah was saying. 'Apparently they had one bride who didn't bother and they had to despatch a dressmaker to tack her up half an hour before she was due at the church.'

Some sort of response seemed to be required and Faith made a superhuman effort to concentrate her mind on what Sarah was saying. 'Try it on.' She repeated the words dully.

'Would you like a hand?' Eager to see the dress, to share the excitement, Sarah lingered, apparently not noticing her distraction.

'Now?'

'Well, the children are having a nap and Harry's gone out so there's no danger of him seeing.' There was some mercy left in heaven, Faith thought. At least she was to be spared his sarcasm. 'Alice was telling me that she's going to be your flower girl. She's terribly excited.'

'Her mother used to come out in a rash when she got over-excited,' Faith warned vaguely. 'I think.'

'Did she? Well, I'll keep an eye on her.'

'If she'll let you.'

'I've discovered that if I pretend to be totally thick and know absolutely nothing she'll deign to help. She actually told me where I could find a spare can of talc for Ben.'

'Obviously that's why I appealed to her. I really am thick, when it comes to babies.' And a few other things.

'Most women are,' Sarah said sympathetically. 'It must be like a nightmare to take a new baby home from the hospital and be expected to get on with it. I had two years' training and they can still surprise me. But of course that won't happen to you.'

Faith froze. Did everyone know the details of her private life? 'What's Debbie been saying?' she demanded.

'Debbie?' Sarah, startled by her fierce reaction, gave an awkward little shrug. 'Nothing. But, well, in your position you'll have a nanny, won't you . . . ?'

In her position? Faith was beginning to feel as though she was losing her grip, but, conscious that Sarah was giving her a rather odd look, she made an effort to pull herself together. 'Shall we do as instructed and check the length of this dress?' she said, changing the subject. 'Before Alice wakes up. She'll want to see her dress, and even if the excitement doesn't bring her out in a rash it might send her temperature up again.'

Sarah showed her the pile of boxes in the hall. 'This must be your dress in the biggest box, and I think that's the one with your bits and pieces — the veil and such-like. We can bring the rest up later.' They carried the two boxes upstairs and Sarah helped to unpack the gown from its layers of lace. 'Oh, Faith,' she sighed. 'It's beautiful.'

It looked, if possible, even more special away from the shop, where it had been seen against dozens of other lace-encrusted gowns. It was a dress for a bride with her heart full of joy, not with this leaden lump that seemed to weigh her down.

'Is there any special underwear to go with it?' Sarah asked.

'A lace basque, but I don't need it now, not just to check the length.'

But Sarah had found the basque buried in a mound of tissue. 'Is this it?' she giggled. 'It's . . . um . . . very sexy. Oh, do put it on so I can see the dress properly.'

Faith made no comment. 'There should be some shoes somewhere. The dress was shortened to go with them.'

'They don't seem to be here. I'll go and have a look downstairs,' Sarah volunteered.

'Thanks.' It was a relief to be on her own, to face up to the truth in the quiet left by Sarah's chatter. She should do it properly. There should be nothing half-hearted . . . unwilling . . . about it. She had chosen to marry Julian. No one was forcing her.

A few minutes later, the basque in place, she stepped into the dress, and, unable to manage more than a couple of the buttons herself, she held it against her and waited for Sarah to return. When she didn't reappear Faith went to the bedroom door and called. There was no reply and she gave a little shrug. She had most probably been diverted by one of the children. Well, she was quite capable of fetching her own shoes, and she picked up the hem of her dress and began to walk in her stockinged feet along the broad band of carpet that softened the hallway.

At the top of the stairs she hesitated, but the entrance hall was empty, the house silent now that the morning staff of cleaners, supervised by Mrs Williams, had done their work. Turning to lift her train, she draped it over her arm and hurried down to the ground floor. She had just seized an armful of boxes when she heard the slightly uneven tread of shoes on the polished floor. She turned to make a dash for the privacy of her bedroom. Too late.

'You seem to be having problems, Faith.' His voice was cool, calculated to infuriate. Well, too bad. She wasn't playing any more. 'Couldn't you wait to try it on?' he pressed. She straightened, clutching the dress against her, aware that her hair had tumbled about her face. She felt half-dressed, ridiculous. 'Would you like me to fasten the rest of the buttons so that you can get the full effect?'

'It isn't necessary,' she said quickly. 'I was looking for my shoes. I'm . . . um . . . just checking the length. I don't want to trip as I walk down the aisle, do I?' She took a step, found she had to lift her skirt, and fumbled the boxes so that they fell, spilling their load of lace and silk at her feet.

'It wouldn't do at all,' Harry agreed impassively. 'So why don't we do it properly?' He scooped up the boxes and their contents and without any apparent difficulty held them secured beneath his arm while he extended his hand. 'The drawing room, I think, would be best.'

His eyes, his voice, were cool, impersonal. Faith hovered between the desire to dash, in the most unladylike fashion, up the stairs to safety, and the opportunity to demonstrate her immunity to Harry March once and for all. The dash was probably wiser, and yet . . . If she ran away from him she was admitting to both of them that he was right and she was wrong. Pride demanded that she show him, demanded that she show herself.

'Thank you, Harry. That's very kind

of you.' She laid her fingers upon his and nothing dreadful happened. Her legs didn't actually turn to jelly. Her heart managed to beat at a fairly consistent rate, although perhaps a little faster than was quite comfortable. Bolder, she continued, 'Sarah was helping, but she seems to have disappeared.'

'Alice came downstairs looking for a drink. She graciously permitted Sarah to help her.' He opened the drawing-room door and stood back to let her through. 'Stand here, in the light.' She obeyed, her feet sinking into the Aubusson carpet as, one by one, Harry began to fasten the loops over the long row of tiny pearl buttons that traced her spine. She was proud of herself. She didn't quiver, she didn't shake. It could have been anyone's knuckles grazing her backbone, anyone's breath cool and sweet on her neck. And yet . . .

'Faith?' Sarah's voice broke into her thoughts.

'In here,' she called. The door opened behind them.

'You've got a visitor . . . Oh!' She sounded shocked. 'I didn't realise Harry was with you. I . . . I'll ask him to wait, shall I?' She sounded far more disturbed than she had that morning when she had discovered them sharing a bed.

'Just one more button and she'll be decent,' Harry said.

'A visitor? Who is it?' Faith turned awkwardly as Harry continued to fiddle with the buttons. There was a man standing in the doorway — slightly above average height, stockily built, with fair hair, a full, soft beard and dark eyes that all too clearly betrayed his shock. For a moment she couldn't believe her own eyes. '*Julian?*' she whispered. 'Is that you?'

'Don't you know?' Harry murmured, his mouth inches from her ear, his hand still possessively on the loop of that last button, holding her captive. He turned from Faith to the man in the doorway

288

as if to say something, then stopped and looked quickly back at her. 'It's true, isn't it? This is the first time you two have actually met.'

10

It was Sarah who found her voice first and broke the silence. 'Out,' she ordered briskly. She bustled around Harry with the determination of a border collie faced with the stubbornest of sheep in an attempt to move him towards the door. 'Don't you know that it's the height of bad luck for the groom to see the bride in her dress before the wedding?'

'Is it?' Harry, ignoring her anxious little gestures, remained where he was. 'Why?'

'It just is,' she said, reluctant to elaborate. But Harry was not to be moved until his curiosity was satisfied. 'It's stupid . . . just an old superstition . . . ' she muttered.

'What superstition?' Julian apparently wanted to know as well, and Sarah turned to him almost with relief, as if she found it easier to explain it to him.

'It's just an old wives' tale. They say that if the groom sees the bride in her dress before the wedding . . . ' she glanced at Harry, then gave a little shrug to show that she for one didn't place any credence in such nonsense ' . . . well, they say the wedding won't ever take place.'

Only Faith saw the look that flashed across Harry's face. Only she was meant to. When he turned to Julian his face was suitably grave.

'You'd think modern women would have better things to do than listen to old — '

'Has my dress come? Can I try it on?' Alice hurtled through the door and skidded to a halt in front of the boxes. Without waiting for an answer she gleefully dived into the piles of tissue-paper.

'No, Alice, not now,' Sarah intervened quickly, making a move to stop her.

But Alice wasn't to be put off that

easily and, spotting Julian, she said, '*He'd* like to see my dress.'

Harry turned to Julian. 'Would you?' He turned to Sarah. 'Or are the bridesmaids included in the same dire predictions?'

'Bridesmaids?' Julian turned to Faith, concern rumpling his forehead. 'How many bridesmaids?'

'Three at the last count.' Harry did not bother to hide his amusement at Julian's obvious dismay and Faith, with Harry's fingers still holding fast to the last button of her dress, remained rooted to the spot with shock, embarrassment, unable to move, to speak, to do anything . . .

'I'm not a bridesmaid, Uncle Harry,' Alice corrected him as she hunted through the boxes. 'I'm a flower girl.'

'I didn't realise . . . ' Julian began. 'I didn't realise you were planning anything quite so formal. I thought, perhaps, the register office — '

'Faith's father is a clergyman,' Harry reminded him. 'You really can't expect her to support the opposition.'

'I . . . I suppose not . . . ' Julian seemed totally bewildered. It was a look she recognised. She had seen it before in men whose whole existence revolved around their work, men who when they lifted their heads from their desks at the end of the day seemed surprised to discover that life had moved on. How much harder must it be for someone who had lived in total isolation with his work not from nine to five but for years?

She turned her head, looked up into Harry's eyes. 'Will you let me go?' she asked. His fingers tightened on the edge of her dress; she could feel his knuckles grazing her backbone. His touch was saying more than words. 'Please.' For the time it took for her racing pulse to beat he continued to hold her and it seemed a lifetime. Then he released her, stood back, leaving her free to choose . . . Except she wasn't free . . . Surely he understood that? She tried, with her eyes, to make him see that she wasn't rejecting him but was met with an impassive stare that told her nothing.

'All done, Faith,' he said. She would never know whether he was talking about the buttons or the spark of passion that had flared so unexpectedly between them. Perhaps it was better that way.

Faith turned and crossed the room to Julian, took his hand . . . 'I can hardly believe it. It's so good to see you,' she said, her eyes filming so that she had to blink hard. After all it was true. She knew him, knew everything he held most dear. It was impossible not to admire him, like him. 'After all this time.' Her smile was warm. Her heart would have to catch up in its own good time.

He looked at their hands, entwined. 'I'm afraid I've come at a bad moment. Timing was never my good point — '

'Just as well you've arrived early,' Harry interrupted tetchily. 'Faith could do with some help with the wedding arrangements. Maybe you can even persuade her to make up her mind about the buffet. At the rate she's going you'll have a hundred and fifty guests — '

'A hundred and fifty?'

'I'm afraid I know a lot of people. And it's a way of repaying lots of little kindnesses to Dad.' She indicated her dress with a slightly embarrassed gesture. 'Look, let me get out of this dress and we can — '

'This isn't my dress!' Having burrowed her way through a mound of tissue-paper, Alice pulled out the long, slinky nightdress, black as night and twice as dangerous, that Harry had tempted her with. 'This is Faith's nightdress. I don't like black,' she said, wrinkling up her nose and turning to appeal to her new-found friend. 'Do you?'

'Well . . . ' he began uncertainly.

'Uncle Harry chose it. He likes — '

'No, sweetheart, I — ' Harry stopped as he realised he was the focus of attention, and Faith's heart sank as she saw the tiniest contraction of the lines fanning out from the navy depths of eyes. 'I . . . er . . . I thought the red one was nicer.' He turned to Julian and shrugged. 'But, like most women, she couldn't make up her mind so she bought them both.'

'Faith's got a pair of red 'jamas too,' Alice informed her new friend confidentially. 'Uncle Harry liked them so much that he bought me a pair.' She stood up to display them for Julian, turning around slowly so that he shouldn't miss the full effect. 'For my birthday,' she prompted, when no exclamation of delight was immediately forthcoming.

Julian, momentarily lost for words, gathered himself. 'Isn't it rather . . . um . . . late to still be wearing pyjamas?'

'Oh, no. You see, I'm sick. In fact,' she said, with the air of someone imparting a great secret, 'you see this?' She pointed to her neck, still slightly swollen. 'It's prob'ly . . . bumps.

'Bumps?'

'She means mumps,' Harry obligingly translated, and watched with interest as Julian visibly paled and took a quick step back to put a safe distance between himself and this source of possible infection.

'And Faith's looking after me while my mummy is away.' She flung herself about Faith's knees and Sarah swooped.

'Faith doesn't want your grubby fingers all over her pretty dress, Alice. And you should be in bed. Come along.' Harry did not take the hint and follow them. In fact, Harry didn't seem in any hurry to depart.

'Can I offer you a bed for the night, Julian?' he enquired smoothly. 'It's a bit chaotic here at the moment, I'm afraid, as you can see, but my sister left me in charge of her brood while she's away.'

'There's more than one?' Julian enquired.

'I could have coped with Alice, but there's a baby, and Faith has kindly stepped into the breach so I'm doing my best to help her with the wedding arrangements. If you stay you could help write the invitations. We're rather behind — '

'I think I'd better put up somewhere. In view of . . . ' He made a vague gesture in the direction of his neck. 'Being isolated for so long leaves one particularly vulnerable to any germ . . . And — um — mumps . . . '

'One can't be too careful — agreed. One hears such things . . . ' Harry was the very soul of understanding.

'You could put up at Mac's,' Faith intervened quickly. 'Have you got a car?'

'No, I came on the train and had to wait a while for a bus.'

'It's quite a walk from the village,' Harry said sympathetically. 'I'll run you down there. He'll find you a room.'

The last thing Faith wanted was Harry going into more details about how helpful he had been with the wedding arrangements, particularly with regard to the trousseau. 'It's all right, Harry; it won't take me a minute to change — '

she began, but Harry waved her back.

'After the effort I've put into doing up all those buttons you'd be better occupied sorting out that dress. Or I'll have to do it again,' he said, in a voice that brooked no argument.

Faith argued, certain now that he was intent on causing mayhem. 'Should you drive? What about your leg? He had a fall yesterday,' she explained to Julian.

'I'll be fine.' Harry eased his leg. 'Although maybe I'll take you up on that offer of a massage later.'

'It will be my pleasure,' Faith replied graciously, but her eyes promised him that he'd be sorry if he did.

Julian, apparently oblivious to the undercurrents, hesitated in the doorway. 'I'll see you later, Faith. For dinner?'

'About eight?' She linked her arm through his and walked with him to the front door, where he turned and held her hand briefly before, deep in thought, following Harry.

Faith waited, but he did not turn

back, and after a moment the shakes finally got the better of her and she subsided into a chair in the drawing room, where, a few minutes later, Sarah found her.

'Faith?'

She looked up.

'I'm sorry, truly. I didn't realise. I just thought Harry was being romantic . . . that he couldn't bear to let you go. I shouldn't have listened to him.'

'Harry? Romantic?' she repeated dully. Then suddenly her attention was caught. 'What did Harry tell you, Sarah?' The girl was flushed, awkward, could hardly meet her eyes. 'You'd better tell me.'

'He said . . . he said . . . '

'Yes?' Faith was losing her patience.

'He said you had a foolish bee in your bonnet about having to organise the wedding from London when you could do it just as well from here.' It all came out in a rush and then Sarah waited, clearly expecting some response, but Faith made no effort to help. 'He tried to catch me at home, stop me coming, but I was at a seminar . . . I told you . . . that was why I couldn't come until late . . . ' Still nothing. She was getting desperate now. 'He said if I made some excuse to leave the moment I arrived he knew you would be suspicious . . . especially after you'd come close to guessing that he had got rid of the first nanny you'd booked — '

'Muriel Kenway?' Faith's voice was dangerously low, dangerously calm as she recalled the moment by the river when she'd known he was trying to distract her, that flash of certainty that he had bought the woman off, her embarrassment at blurting it out . . . No wonder she had got off so lightly. She had just been so grateful that he hadn't started to tease her. That alone should have made her suspicious . . .

'He sounded so reasonable, Faith. It never occurred to me . . . I just assumed . . . '

Faith turned on Sarah. 'What did you assume?'

'Well . . . that you were marrying Harry. What else?'

What else indeed? After all, she had been here alone with Harry; Sarah had found her curled up asleep beside him that very morning. No wonder she hadn't been shocked. Even the fact that his niece was going to be her flower girl . . .

Alice. Just how far . . . ? 'And did he make Alice pretend she didn't like you?' she asked dangerously. 'Or was that just luck?'

'Oh, just luck,' Sarah said, quickly. 'At least . . . Oh, dear, you don't really think he put her up to it, do you?'

'Why not? The pair of them are as thick as thieves. And I did wonder where Alice had managed to find a frog. Do you think her temperature was an act too?' She recalled guiltily that she was the one who had shown Alice exactly how to frighten the grown-ups.

'Oh, no. Really,' Sarah said, flustered. 'That wasn't acting. Harry was distraught.' She hesitated, then placed her hand on Faith's arm. 'He's in love with you; I'm sure of it.'

'Love?' What was the matter with everyone? Had they all overdosed on *Cinderella*? 'Stuff and nonsense,' she said gruffly. 'I was just a challenge and he never could resist a challenge.' Sarah gave her an old-fashioned look, clearly unconvinced. 'He told me so himself.'

'Well, if nothing happened . . . '

Nothing beyond a few kisses, an uncomfortably heightened pulse rate. But he had blown on the embers of her emotions, stirred them into life, reminding her . . . reminding her . . . 'Nothing happened, Sarah.' From somewhere Faith managed a reassuring smile, covered Sarah's hand with her own. 'Don't worry. No harm done,' she said, with a forced brightness. 'Now, shall we try and find my shoes? I might as well try them on since Harry's gone to the trouble of fastening all these buttons.'

'And the very least I can do is stick around to help you unfasten them.' Sarah grinned. 'Unless you'd rather

303

wait for Harry to help you? It would just serve him right.'

Faith laughed obediently, although underneath she was jelly. Just how far would he have taken his game? she wondered, then stopped herself. Rather more to the point, surely, was the kind of resistance she would have put up? When it came to passion versus companionship she had the feeling that common sense wouldn't stand a chance. Harry must never be allowed to get that close again.

'The hem is perfect,' Sarah said, reclaiming her attention. 'The dress is perfect. You'll make a beautiful bride. Now, I think you'd better come upstairs before I undo you.'

She was halfway across the hall when Harry's shadow fell across her. Sarah took one look at his face and beat a retreat up the stairs, mumbling something about the children.

'Did Mac find Julian a room?'

'A quiet single at the back.'

He was *still* doing it, still tormenting

her! And finally she snapped. 'How could you, Harry?'

'It was all he had left.' His innocent air didn't fool Faith for one moment and she flung her fist at his shoulder, catching him by surprise, knocking him off balance. 'Hey! What — ?'

'I'm not talking about hotel rooms.'

'Then what are you talking about?' He saw the second blow coming and sidestepped it, infuriating her still further.

'Oh, pick any one from five, Harry, but let's start with your favourite subject — lingerie. You preferred the red one, did you?' She struck out again. It was a mistake. This time he caught her wrist and pulled her towards him, holding her close so that her arms were pinned between them and she couldn't move.

'You know I did,' he rasped. She trembled as his arms held her close, at the sweet softness of his breath on her hair, the rasp of his chin against her temple. She so desperately wanted to stop fighting him, to dissolve in his arms, but she couldn't, mustn't. So she flung her head back and continued to lash at him with her tongue.

'So why did you stop with the nightdress, Harry? You said yourself you'd never seen such an entertaining selection of underwear. I'm surprised you didn't bring it all out, piece by piece, since you were enjoying yourself so much — ' He stopped the angry invective by clamping his hand over her mouth.

'No, Faith,' he said harshly, his eyes slaty, unreadable. 'I was not enjoying myself. I don't suppose you'll believe this but I can't remember the last time I had less fun.' He took his hand from her mouth, raked his fingers back through his hair, as if almost embarrassed by the depth of the feelings she had aroused in him. 'Not that it would have bothered Julian if I had. If I'd found someone buttoning up my bride's dress I'd have — '

'Hit him?'

'Probably,' he admitted.

'Julian isn't like that.'

'Julian didn't even notice what was going on.'

'Nothing was going — ' She was shouting and she forced herself to stop. 'Nothing was going on,' she said quietly. Nothing she wanted to think about. 'How did you persuade Miss Kenway she wasn't needed?' she demanded, changing the subject.

'Muriel Kenway was a pushover. An old romantic.'

'Like Sarah?'

'Like everyone but you. Although I was beginning to hope — ' She was leaning away from him but there was nowhere else to go, and the fierce curve of his mouth was almost on hers, sensual, passionate. It was that rare kind of mouth that would look good in close-up on a wide screen, perfect but for a tiny scar . . .

She caught her breath and pushed hard, staggering away from him. 'Sarah had an excuse,' she said angrily. 'She thought she was playing Cupid, not helping you in some game you'd devised for your own amusement, but I know you better. Tell me, Harry, just what *was* the plan? Did Aunt Janet ask you to use your charm to wreck the wedding?'

'Wreck it? I can see why she might not approve of you marrying a man you've never met, who has convinced you that you haven't the right to a family of your own, but why would she choose me to create havoc?'

'Oh, she thinks *you're* irresistible . . . '

'How wrong can one woman be?'

Wrong? *Wrong?* Didn't he know how close he'd come? 'And then you decided to make me look like . . . like . . . '

His forehead contracted in a frown. 'Like what, Faith?'

'Like the kind of girl who lets just any man choose her underwear!'

The frown disappeared. 'On the contrary, darling, if you'd listened to me you'd have bought long johns.'

'Well, maybe I will,' she declared. 'Maybe I will.' And to her chagrin she burst into tears before turning and rushing up to her room.

★   ★   ★

A tap at the door stirred her out of a distant contemplation of her wardrobe. Having slept in her good trousers and silk shirt, she only had her skirt and her dribbled-on jeans to wear.

The tap was repeated and she stirred. Harry was standing in the doorway and for a moment, for one crazy moment, she thought he was going to apologise. But he didn't. Instead he crossed the room and opened one of the wardrobes. 'I don't suppose you have anything to wear tonight. Julian might be a bit slow on the uptake but he could hardly miss you wearing one of my shirts, could he?'

She didn't answer.

'Elizabeth usually leaves something behind and she's about the same size as you.'

She wasn't sure whether to hit him or cry. Or both. But she kept a stiff hold on her face, refusing to let it show what she was feeling.

'I phoned Mac and asked him to lay on something special for tonight,' he continued stiffly. 'Your man's probably got a ring burning a hole in his pocket and he'll want to ask you to marry him properly, with lobster and champagne.'

He turned, and because she was afraid he could read her face all too well she replied equally stiffly. 'I'm sure we'll think of some way to pass the time.'

'Faith, don't — ' he began, halfway across the room to her.

'Uncle Harry?' They turned as one to see Alice standing in the doorway, a circle of peach rosebuds perched lopsidedly on her head. 'Can I phone Mummy and tell her about being Faith's flower girl?'

Harry seemed frozen, unable to answer. Faith rescued him — rescued herself. 'What a lovely idea, Alice,' she said, quickly moving over to the child, out of the dangerous gravitational pull that seemed to draw her always into

Harry's arms. 'She'd love to hear all about your dress. Why don't you hop into bed? I'm sure Uncle Harry will let you use his mobile.'

The child looked at Harry. 'Can I?'

'Of course, sweetheart,' he said, his voice ragged as he turned away. 'I'll fetch it for you.' He didn't look back as he left the room.

Mention of the phone brought her father rushing back to Faith's mind. She still hadn't spoken to him, but there was no hurry; it was perfectly obvious why he had rung her. He had been ringing to give her the good news that Julian had come home early.

She gave a little sniff, found her handkerchief, had a good blow. This was ridiculous. She hadn't wept since Michael had walked out on her, left her to pick up the pieces of her young life. Well, she'd picked them up, put them back together again. She had a successful career and now she was going to marry a man she liked and respected. What woman could ask for more? And, if tears had caught her out twice in one day, well, it was nothing but pre-wedding nerves.

★ ★ ★

She fastened up her hair, automatically teasing out the tendrils to curl at her temples. She made up her face, fitted her simple gold earrings. She slipped into her sandals and whirled before the mirror in Elizabeth's dress, the fuchsia silk chiffon floating as if defying gravity. Julian couldn't fail to be impressed. And Harry? Harry, she told herself, didn't matter. Mustn't matter.

But as she descended the staircase the great oak door of the manor was standing wide open and Harry's silhouette was outlined against the evening sunshine. He turned as he heard her hesitant step, his face in shadow, and for a moment said nothing, then he stepped to one side to let her pass.

'I've brought your car round to the front.'

'Thank you.'

'It's a shame it clashes so horribly with that dress. I thought I saw a black one — '

'I'm not in mourning. And don't bother to wait up for me.' It was a cheap remark, but she needed to retaliate, to punish him for making her feel so torn.

He must have known, because he stopped her, his hand so light on her wrist that she barely felt it. 'You can fool yourself, Faith, you might even be able to fool Julian, but you can't fool me.'

'I don't know what you're talking about.'

He took her chin and turned it so that she was forced to face him. 'Yes, you do. You know that ten minutes after I set eyes on you I wanted to carry you off to my bed — '

'*Ten minutes?*' she exploded.

' — and you wanted me to.' They glared at each other. Then Harry shrugged. 'Julian, on the other hand, is planning to marry you and he wouldn't even kiss you in case he caught Alice's 'bumps'.'

It wasn't that. Julian wasn't like Harry. He was reserved, shy; he could never have kissed her publicly. 'Even you managed to stop yourself from making a pass for, what . . . twenty-four hours?' she retaliated.

'Are you saying you didn't enjoy the experience?' His finger stopped her lips. 'If you lie, I'll tell Janet.'

She brushed his hand away. 'Do your worst. I'm too old to be sent to my room.'

'I promise it would be more fun than dinner.'

She was unable to resist the temptation to dent such arrogance. 'Julian is all the company I need.'

'Your nose will grow,' he warned her, then gave a careless little shrug. 'Well, I'm sure with a little encouragement he'll warm up, but he's been in cold storage a long time, Faith. It might take a little time.'

'Earlier today you suggested I'd be fighting off a ravening sex maniac,' she reminded him.

'That was before I met him.' He took her hand and dropped her keys into her palm, closing her trembling fingers about them, the leather fob and the metal still warm from his touch.

* * *

Mac did them proud with a secluded table in a corner overlooking the river, and there were flowers and candles on the table. Julian smiled a touch awkwardly as he took his seat opposite her and for a moment neither of them spoke.

'Your photograph really doesn't do you justice . . . ' he began.

'You've had your beard trimmed . . . ' She couldn't think of anything else to say.

They stopped, laughed a little. 'I'm sorry I wasn't at home when you arrived, Julian. I think Dad must have

315

tried to let me know but we had something of a crisis last night with Alice — '

'The mumps?'

'Just swollen glands.'

'I'm afraid I rather panicked. Stupid of me, I suppose.'

'No. You were right. There can be complications.' There was a pause. 'Tell me your latest news on the project,' she encouraged. 'Why have you come home early? Did your research grant run out sooner than expected?'

He hesitated, looked at his hand. 'It was to do with money,' he agreed.

'It's such a pity. I know how much your work means to you. Is there any chance that it will continue?'

'One way or another.'

'Good.' Another pause. 'Well, I've got a bundle of house details for the Cambridge area. I was going to visit the area for a couple of days next week. Now you're here we can go together.' He seemed to be miles away. 'Only if you want to,' she assured him. 'I expect

316

you've got a lot of things to do . . . ' She waited for some response and he looked at her, made an effort to come back from wherever he had been in his head.

'No. I'll be happy to accompany you. I just hadn't realised you were going to arrange the wedding so soon.'

'Well, you agreed that there wasn't any point in waiting, and my father is going to New Zealand for six months on an ecumenical exchange at the end of August.'

'Oh, I see. Of course.'

'I wrote and told you. And about my plans for a consultancy. Now I've left the bank I can't wait to get started — '

'You've given up your job?'

'That's why my aunt was able to blackmail me into helping Harry. She used to be Harry's nanny so she was first choice, but she's having a hip replacement so . . . ' She was talking too much. It was nerves. 'I don't suppose my letter reached you before you left base,' she finished lamely.

'No.'

'Julian, is something wrong? You look terribly pale.'

'Wrong?' he repeated dully, then roused himself. 'What ever could be wrong, my dear? I'm sorry I'm not terribly bright — still a touch jet-lagged, I expect.' He reached across and took her hands in his. 'You looked very beautiful in your wedding dress.'

'You shouldn't have seen it. Tempting fate.' She tried a smile. 'It's just as well neither of us is superstitious.'

'No, indeed.' He answered her smile. 'Although I confess I could never bring myself to walk under a ladder.'

Faith gave a little shudder at the thought. 'Oh, no. Or put new shoes on the table.'

'And I always find myself throwing a little spilt salt over my shoulder.' His smile deepened. 'It's certainly a good thing that neither of us is superstitious.' Faith laughed out loud. Encouraged, Julian stroked his beard. 'Do you expect me to wear a top hat? I'm not sure it will go with this.'

'You could always shave it off.'

'It helps to keep the face protected against the cold.'

'East Anglia isn't the Antarctic.' Her laughter faltered as she remembered Harry's warning.

'But — No, of course it isn't. And maybe you're right. It's a symbol of my bachelor past and should go.' He raised his hand to summon a waiter. 'I'm afraid I haven't had time to look for a ring for you, Faith, so I can't do this properly, but I think now is the moment to toast the future . . . '

The evening was pleasant. The food was excellent; the champagne made them both a little silly. And when he walked her to her car Julian took her hand. 'May I kiss you?'

She swallowed, foolishly nervous. She had little experience of being asked permission before a man kissed her. Michael and Harry had that in common too. They both knew when she wanted to be kissed, even when she didn't know herself.

There was a moment's awkwardness, then a tentative, bristly touching of lips. It didn't send her pulse racing, or make her go weak at the knees, but then she had never expected it to. And no doubt in time he would get the knack of it.

11

Faith didn't drive straight back to the manor. Instead she drove up through the woods until she came to a small clearing. The short summer night had not quite claimed the sky and a gibbous moon laid a silver halo over the trees. She scarcely noticed, but sat on the grass, her arms wrapped about her knees, and stared at nothing.

'Is this a private party, or can anyone join in?' She'd heard Harry's slightly uneven footsteps coming up the hill and now she turned her head on her knees to look at him.

'How did you know where I was?' she asked as he sat beside her, taking care to keep a safe distance between them.

'You did the electronic equivalent of stepping on a twig.' He picked up a twig and demonstrated, breaking it with a sharp crack. 'You set off an alarm.'

She looked around. 'I didn't see anything.'

'You weren't supposed to. I test new equipment all over the estate. I could tell you where every badger has its sett, every fox has its earth.'

'I bet you don't get poachers,' she said.

'No. My pheasants only have to contend with marauding foxes and egg-stealing stoats.' He looked at her. 'Do you want to talk about it, Faith?'

She shook her head. 'There's nothing to talk about.'

Harry, elbows on knees, stirred the ground with the twig. 'I hoped he'd be a wimp. An irritating know-it-all. Someone I could loathe. I should have known better. You're far too sensible to marry someone who isn't thoroughly nice.' As Harry distractedly raked his fingers through his hair the moonlight gleamed on the pale skin inside his wrist and Faith yearned to reach out, kiss that vulnerable spot, feel the heat of his blood pounding in his pulse, so that he would know that in some place hidden deep within her she would always love him. Hardly the thoughts of a sensible woman. 'Will you be happy?' Harry turned and she looked quickly away.

'As happy as I expected to be.' At least, as happy as she'd expected to be a week ago. Before Harry had kissed her. Before she had held Ben in her arms, cuddled Alice and remembered that long before she had been levelheaded and sensible she had known what love was and that her only ambition had been to be a wife, a mother. This feeling she had for Harry felt terribly similar and her throat ached with the tears she was holding back. But Michael had taught her not to trust in such fleeting emotions. The tears had passed then. They would again.

'I could check him out for you,' Harry offered. 'Who knows what dark secrets he might have hidden away.'

'Secrets?' She managed a laugh. 'Like what?'

'He could be a bigamist,' Harry offered.

'You're not serious?'

'Or divorced. That would explain why he'd rather not have a church wedding.'

'He isn't divorced.'

'What about a passel of illegitimate children?' She gave him a cool look. 'Unlikely,' he agreed, a little jaggedly.

Faith jumped to her feet, turning away so that the moonlight would not betray that her eyes were over-bright. 'Please stop. Julian is a thoroughly good and kind man and he doesn't deserve this.' The twig Harry had been holding snapped again with a sharp crack and suddenly he was behind her, his hands on her shoulders, and she could feel his warmth stealing about her.

'No, he doesn't. Reconsider, Faith, before it's too late. Julian thinks you're a sensible, level-headed young woman who will make him a sensible, level-headed wife.'

'And you know better?'

324

His grip tightened. 'I could show you. I could make it impossible for you to marry him; we both know that.' His body was imprinted against her, warm, tempting. She caught her lower lip to keep from crying out. 'Admit it, Faith,' he demanded.

'Yes,' she whispered. 'I know it.'

'But you'd hate me and I couldn't live with that.' He turned her to face him and wiped the treacherous tears from her cheeks with the pad of his thumb before holding her close, so that she could hear the steady thumping of his heart, feel his strength enfolding her. How could she ever hate him? The truth was that ever since she'd met Harry March her well-ordered existence had been tumbling about her ears like a card house, and another moment out beneath the stars might yet undo her resolve to hold to her promise whatever the cost.

She sniffed, took the handkerchief that Harry offered. 'I seem to have lost my head in the last few days. It's

325

nothing serious,' she declared, with only the tiniest tremble in her voice to betray her. Somehow his hands had remained against her cheeks, cradling her face, but she didn't have the strength to protest any more. 'I'll recover the minute I get back to London,' she said, more to herself than him.

'Will you, my love? I'm sure you'll try. You'll live in a house that's never quite warm enough, use low-energy bulbs that are never quite bright enough, drive your neighbours mad with your plans for recycling every scrap of rubbish in your area and go everywhere by bicycle — '

'What's wrong with that?'

'Wrong? Oh, nothing very much, I suppose. I'm sure you'll do it the same way you do everything. With great thoroughness. You'll probably write pamphlets about how to save energy, maybe even become a television pundit — '

'Don't! That does sound dreadful!'

'Does it? Far worse is the prospect of you ending up as a sort of universal

aunt, godmother to all your friends'
children because, although you'll long
for babies of your own, you've been
brainwashed, for the noblest of motives,
into thinking it would be selfish to
produce any of your — '

From somewhere she found the
strength to step back, break the contact,
put a yard of distance between them.
'When is Elizabeth coming home?' she
cut in sharply.

'You're so eager to whisk Julian away
to East Anglia to look at houses?'
Eager? Not eager. A touch desperate,
perhaps. 'She'll be back tomorrow,
Faith. She hoped you would stay long
enough to meet her so that she could
thank you herself.'

'Of course.' She took a step in the
direction of her car, then turned back.
'Can I give you a lift, Harry?'

'I want the rest of your life and you
offer me a lift.' He shook his head, and
before she could say another word he
had disappeared into the darkness of
the night.

Elizabeth and her husband, his neck in a collar and his arm in a plaster, arrived home the next afternoon. In a whirl of excitement Alice hurled herself into her mother's arms and hugged her until she begged for mercy. Then Elizabeth saw Ben and, crooning soft, loving words, she took him from Faith's arms, leaving her feeling cold and empty.

She hadn't seen Harry since their meeting in the wood. He had gone by the time she had woken, leaving early to collect his sister and brother-in-law from the airport. Now he caught Faith's eye. 'Motherhood,' he murmured coolly. 'It gets them all in the end.'

Elizabeth laughed, tears sparkling in her blue eyes, as she looked up. 'I pity men, don't you? Missing this?' She didn't wait for an answer, assuming acquiescence. 'Thank you so much for coming to poor Harry's assistance. You're an angel, Faith.'

'Some angel,' Harry muttered. 'She

didn't know one end of a baby from the other — '

'It didn't take me long to learn,' Faith said, turning quickly to Elizabeth. 'Alice was an enormous help. I don't know what I would have done without her.' Alice, overcome by a sudden attack of shyness, clung to her mother's skirts. 'But now you're home I feel I can leave with a clear conscience.' She glanced nervously at Harry, wondering what other tricks he might have up his sleeve to delay her.

'There's no need to rush away, is there?' It was Elizabeth, intercepting the look, who encouraged her to linger. 'Can't you stay for dinner? Harry's told me how kind you've been — '

Harry, it seemed, never missed a trick.

'I'm afraid Julian is waiting for me. He has to get back to London tonight. A meeting — '

'Oh, I see.' She didn't give up that easily. 'How is Janet? I must make an effort — '

'Don't harass the girl, Elizabeth; she's been delayed on our behalf for long enough. You'll see Janet at Faith's wedding.' The warning tone was clear enough.

'Of course.' She glanced uncertainly at Harry. 'So kind of you to ask Alice — '

'Why don't you take Mummy upstairs and show her your dress, Alice?' Harry intervened smoothly. 'I'm sure she can't wait to see it.'

'No, no, indeed,' Elizabeth said, seizing the opportunity to leave them together. 'And I'd better check to see how John's coping.' She took Faith's hand. 'Goodbye, Faith, and thank you again.'

'Goodbye, Elizabeth.' Faith turned to Harry, and after a moment's hesitation offered him her hand. 'Goodbye, Harry.'

He ignored it. 'I have a present for you.'

'A present?'

'A wedding present.' He retrieved a shiny white box from the hall table.

'What is it?'

'Something useful. Don't open it

now.' He bent forward, brushing her cheek with his lips, and fighter squadrons of butterflies flew in formation across her abdomen. 'Goodbye, Faith.'

'Goodbye, Harry.' And she meant it. Despite the butterflies, and despite the fact that her renowned level-headedness had taken a severe beating in the last few days, she hadn't quite lost her wits. Julian might seem unexciting alongside Harry March, but then who wouldn't? Marriage wasn't the moonlight and roses of fairy tales, and what happened when the white heat of passion cooled? Marriage was a series of small compromises; it was the give and take of everyday life that made it work.

A small voice inside her whispered that she could have had it all and, as she paused for one last moment on the steps of Wickham Hall, listening to Alice's shrieks of laughter drifting out of the first-floor window, remembering how Ben had felt lying warm and snug in her arms as she'd fed him, she felt a terrible hunger deep within her. But she had accepted Julian on the terms he had offered. She couldn't back out now. She knew how it felt to be jilted by someone you loved, someone you trusted. She lifted her head and, taking a deep breath, climbed into her car, putting the box Harry had given her on the passenger seat.

She eyed it through suspiciously watery eyes and, after a moment's hesitation, opened the lid. Inside, nestling in layers of tissue, was a set of fine silk thermal underwear: a vest with long sleeves, a pair of long johns and socks. A card dropped onto her lap as she shook it out. 'To keep you warm on your bicycle. And anywhere else you might need it. Harry.'

Just for a moment her breath caught in her throat and the tears threatened to overwhelm her. Crossly, she brushed them away and dumped the underwear back in its box. How typical of the man to insist on having the last word.

★ ★ ★

The bridesmaids had already left for the church, were walking the few yards across the churchyard, taking Alice, chattering excitedly, with them. Now it was her turn.

It had been a rush; she had been too busy emptying her flat, selling her car, organising everything down to the last pin to think about Harry or babies or anything, and for that, at least, she had been grateful. Julian, too, had been busy — giving talks, visiting fellow scientists, working on a paper, putting the finishing touches to a book he had written, so that, he had told her, he could concentrate on their honeymoon. She gave a little shiver.

'Are you cold, Faith?' Her father voiced his concern.

'No. Just nervous. All brides are nervous; surely you must know that?'

'I've never quite understood why. Unless they're afraid the bridegroom won't show? This one doesn't strike me as a bolter.'

'Dad!'

Her father gave her a gently teasing smile. 'That was supposed to make you laugh, Faith.' She tried, but couldn't quite make it, and he frowned. 'Michael was so long ago . . . '

'I know. Silly, isn't it?' She gave an awkward little shrug. 'Perhaps if he had told me himself, explained, I could have understood. But to just write a letter. It was so . . . cold-blooded.'

'He didn't write it.' Faith turned to her father, her face creased in confusion. He gave an awkward little shrug. 'That is, I'm almost certain he didn't write it. I suppose I should have told you before but I was so glad to see the back of him . . . '

'I don't understand.'

'You went to stay with Janet for a few days before the wedding, remember? I'm pretty sure his mother took the opportunity to tell him you'd changed your mind. No doubt she produced something convincing; maybe she even went to the expense of buying another ring to give him back.'

'But . . . why? Why would Michael believe her?'

'She only agreed to the wedding because she was convinced you were pregnant. Do you remember the way you bounced into our polite little tea-party and announced that you were getting married and if we tried to stop you you would live together anyway?'

Of course she remembered. She remembered it all. She remembered how, after that first time, she had lain in Michael's arms utterly happy, full of what they would do with their life together. Michael had said her father would never agree to their marriage, not until she'd finished university. It had been her idea to shock them into saying yes and, swept along by her own cleverness, she had sprung it on them without bothering to discuss it with Michael first; after all, why should they wait just because their parents thought she should have a degree? What possible use would a degree in economics be to someone who was going to spend the rest of her life raising babies?

Faith stared at her bouquet, not seeing the peach rosebuds; for the first time since Michael had bolted she wondered if he had ever wanted to marry her. Had he simply been cornered by her frankness? He'd bedded the vicar's virginal daughter and he could hardly say his intentions were anything but honourable . . .

'Poor Michael. I don't suppose he needed much persuading when his mother offered him a way out. He was probably glad of the opportunity to escape.'

'Maybe. He always was weak . . . '

Compared with Harry. Compared with Julian. She could see that now. Why hadn't she been able to see it before? Maybe that was what people had meant when they'd said she was too young.

'You're a bit pale,' her father said, looking anxiously towards the church. 'Do you want to delay this for a few minutes?'

She pulled herself together, managed

a smile. 'No. There's no need. Really. I've kept Julian waiting quite long enough.'

'Well, a little late is expected, but more than ten minutes does suggest cold feet,' her father agreed.

'Perhaps I should be wearing my thermal socks . . . ' she murmured as she turned to pick up her train. The errant thought brought Harry so vividly to mind that for a moment she could almost hear him laughing . . .

'What was that?'

'Nothing, Dad. Nothing at all.'

The sun was warm as they crossed the churchyard and there was a flurry of activity as Alice and the bridesmaids took their places. Then the organist began to play Wagner's bridal march and there was no more time to think. She heard the congregation rise to its feet, and a kind of collective gasp as she began the long, slow walk towards Julian waiting at the far end of the aisle, catching glimpses through her veil of the faces of neighbours, friends, people she had known all her life, Aunt Janet, her wheelchair bedecked with white ribbons — all smiling with approval at Harry's choice of wedding dress.

She could feel her throat tightening as her father surrendered her to Julian. She shouldn't be thinking of Harry, not now. Please, not now.

'Dearly beloved . . . ' She concentrated fiercely on the beautiful words of the service — anything to shut out the memory of tormenting blue eyes. ' . . . duly considering the causes for which Matrimony was ordained.

'First, It was ordained for the procreation of children . . . '

Children? She turned to Julian; he met her eyes, looked away quickly, and a tiny gasp escaped her lips. *He had known.* That was why, honest man that he was, he hadn't wanted a church wedding. But he was going ahead with it anyway, for her sake. She closed her eyes. She should have remembered the words. How many times had she heard them as a choirgirl? Hundreds. Had she deliberately blanked them out?

The Dean moved smoothly on and she forced herself to concentrate. This was her wedding ' . . . these two persons present come now to be joined. Therefore if any man can shew any just cause, why they may not lawfully be joined together, let him now speak or else hereafter for ever hold his peace.'

He paused, looked up from his prayer book, waited. There was a moment's silence. Purely a formality. No one, least of all the Dean, expected someone to stand up, declare an impediment, but Faith wanted to shout out that it was all a terrible lie — that they shouldn't be getting married, not like this. The sudden clatter of the huge iron door-handle was almost a relief as the tension broke and everyone jumped.

'I hope I'm not too late to stop this.' Harry's voice rang out from the back of the church. 'But I've discovered something terribly important — something Faith should know.'

Faith heard the congregation turn as

one in their seats, the sudden murmur of concerned voices, and slowly she, too, turned her head. Harry was outlined in the doorway of the church, a dark silhouette against the bright sunshine.

The Dean, who had never had anything like this happen in thirty years of ministry, was clearly at something of a loss. He beckoned to Faith's father. 'I think we'd better . . . um . . . adjourn to the vestry,' he whispered.

'There's no need. Really.' Faith had never been so angry in all her life. How could Harry do such a thing? Julian was a good man. Kind. Loving. He didn't deserve this. 'Ignore him,' she said.

But the Dean had recovered his wits and wasn't to be put off. 'No, really, my dear. The young man must be heard.'

Faith turned slowly to face Julian. 'I'm sorry . . . ' she murmured as Harry's uneven footsteps echoed around the vaulted roof. 'I'm so sorry.'

The Dean indicated the way to the vestry, but Harry stopped him.

'I don't want anyone to think that

there is something here that should be hidden. What I have to say shames no one.'

'But then . . . ?'

'What is it, Harry?' Faith demanded.

'It's taken days of poking about, but I finally managed to contact someone from the Antarctic survey this morning. Faith, I know why Julian came back to England two weeks early.'

'No!' It was Julian who tried to stop him.

'The project ran out of money,' Faith interjected furiously. 'You know that.'

'On the contrary, my dear,' Harry said. 'Global warming has become a hot political potato and suddenly Julian has more research funding than he knows what to do with. The reason he came racing down to Wickham Ash was to explain that the wedding would have to be postponed, indefinitely, because he was going back the moment the money was safe in the bank.'

'*What?*' Faith turned to Julian. 'Is this true?' One look at his face assured her that it was. 'Why didn't you tell me?'

Harry answered for him. 'Because when he arrived he was confronted with a girl dressed in her bridal finery, eagerly organising a posse of brides-maids, writing invitations and deciding on the menu for a reception for a hundred and fifty people. A girl who had already given up her job and had begun to look for a house.'

'Yes, but . . . ' Faith turned to Julian. 'You would have sacrificed your research work, everything you held most dear, just so that I shouldn't be disappointed?'

'I asked you to marry me, Faith. When I saw . . . Well, I couldn't let you down.'

'Tell him he can go, Faith. Let him get back to work.'

'There's no need,' Julian said stiffly.

'Your nobility does you credit, but don't be a chump,' Harry said. 'You can be godfather to our first child if it makes you feel better.'

Julian looked from Harry to Faith

and back again. 'You mean . . . Oh, good grief . . . ' Relief swept across his face. 'You were making your own sacrifice to keep your promise to me?'

'Two chumps,' Harry agreed.

Julian leaned forward and kissed Faith's cheek before taking her hand and placing it in Harry's. 'I promise you I'm not normally so slow, Harry. My only excuse is that my heart was still thousands of miles away on the ice. Be happy, both of you.'

'Well, Harry March,' Aunt Janet scolded, wheeling her chair to the chancel steps, 'you cut that a bit fine. That bump on your head has slowed you down.'

'It's not that easy getting hold of someone in the Antarctic.'

'Humph.' She spun her wheelchair around. 'Well, I don't know what you're all sitting here for,' she informed the stunned congregation. 'The show's over for today. But since it's a pity to waste good food I suggest we get on with the party.' She looked up at Julian. 'Are you coming, young man?'

'Well, actually, if you'll excuse me . . . '
he glanced at his watch, then turned to
Faith's father ' . . . there's a flight . . . If
I could use the vicarage telephone?'

'Help yourself,' he invited bemusedly.

'What about you two?' Janet demanded.

'I think we'll give this one a miss,
Janet,' Harry said. 'It'll give everyone a
chance to talk about us and we've more
important things to do.'

'Like what?' Faith demanded.

'We've a wedding to arrange, and this
time I'll do the organising to make sure
nothing goes wrong at the last minute.'

'A wedding? You must be joking. I'm
never going through anything like this
again,' she declared, pulling off her veil.
Debbie rescued it.

'Third time lucky,' Janet Bridges
called back as her brother wheeled her
away down the aisle. 'And once word of
this gets around they'll be fighting for
invitations on the black market.'

'Oh, wonderful,' Faith murmured.

'Besides, you've no choice,' Harry

added. 'You promised Alice she could be your flower girl.' He touched her lips with the tip of his finger. 'And a promise is a promise. So unless you've got someone else lined up, Faith Bridges, you're going to have to marry me before she grows out of her dress. What do you say?'

'Is that a proposal?'

'You know it is. And if you think I'm getting down on one knee you can think again.'

'Poor old crock,' she teased, leaning into the curve of his arm. 'How did you guess, Harry? About Julian?'

'His eyes were somewhere else. On a distant horizon. Mine used to be there. I know how it feels.'

'But not now?'

'I promise you, Faith, that for the rest of my life my horizon will only ever be you.' He kissed the fine blue tracery of veins at her temple and she lifted her face to his, almost drowning in the intensity of love blazing from his eyes. Then he led her down the aisle and out into the sunshine.

Parked on a skew at the lych-gate, door still flung open where Harry had made his dash to the church, was a low red sports car with a soft black hood — the same car that last week she'd sold to a middle-aged gentleman with a military moustache who'd told her he collected classic sports cars . . .

'But that's my — '

'I had a feeling you'd be needing it. But I can see a traffic warden heading this way so I think we'd better move it.' He tucked her into the passenger seat, folding her train about her feet, pausing only to place a lingering kiss on her upturned lips. 'I was right about that dress. You can get another just like it for our wedding . . . No rush . . . any time within the next few weeks . . . Elizabeth is getting impatient.' He grinned. 'And so am I.'

'I didn't say yes,' she reminded him, then as he accelerated away towards the motorway and the vicarage disappeared from view she had more urgent concerns. 'Where are we going, Harry? I haven't any clothes with me.'

'Don't worry about it, my darling.' He turned to her and his face creased in a heart-stopping smile. 'I don't anticipate you'll be needing any for the immediate future.'

Faith opened her mouth to object, then closed it again. Irresistible, her aunt had said. And who was arguing?

THE END

We do hope that you have enjoyed reading this large print book.

Did you know that all of our titles are available for purchase?

We publish a wide range of high quality large print books including: **Romances, Mysteries, Classics General Fiction Non Fiction and Westerns**

Special interest titles available in large print are: **The Little Oxford Dictionary Music Book, Song Book Hymn Book, Service Book**

Also available from us courtesy of Oxford University Press: **Young Readers' Dictionary (large print edition) Young Readers' Thesaurus (large print edition)**

For further information or a free brochure, please contact us at: **Ulverscroft Large Print Books Ltd., The Green, Bradgate Road, Anstey, Leicester, LE7 7FU, England. Tel:** (00 44) **0116 236 4325 Fax:** (00 44) **0116 234 0205**

VERA'S VENTURE

Anne Holman

World War II is over, but new problems confront Vera. Her wartime job ends, and her husband Geoff is invalided out of the army and needs work. With two young children they must leave their home and move into a rundown cottage in Norfolk. Geoff has taken an engineering job with the Fen River Board. And whilst the river banks desperately need strengthening, floods are threatening the flat Fenlands, and Vera must protect her family.

DARK FORTUNE

Susan Udy

A lottery win changes everything for Kate: even her closest friend resents her luck. So, she starts a new life elsewhere, keeping her fortune a secret. However, it's soon apparent that someone who knows the truth is subjecting her to a campaign of fear. Kate doesn't know which of her new friends to trust. Could it be Dan, her attractive neighbour; Irene, who swiftly befriends her; or the more disturbing Fergal? Or could it be someone from her past?

MOUNTAIN SHADOWS

Paula Williams

When Jenna Manning's mother dies, she makes a series of shocking discoveries. She learns that her mother had cut her out of her will . . . but then finds that, along with the thriller writer Luke Grantley, she's part-owner of the family's old home in Cumbria. Jenna decides to visit 'Brackwith' and finds the injured Luke in residence. But it's only after stumbling upon the truth about her father, that Jenna and Luke realise their lives have become completely entwined.

DREAMING OF LOVE

Fay Cunningham

Alice first meets Leo Grant late at night in the local supermarket. Unfortunately, she is wearing bunny pyjamas and a woolly hat — not exactly the outfit she would normally choose to impress a famous American author, particularly when he is with a gorgeous redhead. Lucy's five-year-old niece thinks Leo Grant is a prince in disguise, straight out of a storybook, and the mysterious redhead is hiding a deadly secret. Alice's world is about to get curiouser and curiouser . . .

A CHANCE ENCOUNTER

Margaret Mounsdon

When Grace Maxwell swerves to avoid a dog that runs out in front of her car, the near miss begins a chain of events that leads her to Daniel Stafford. At the college ball, Melissa Harper, Daniel's fiancée, had discovered Grace and Daniel kissing, and she had broken off their engagement . . . Grace now works as a vet's receptionist and to make matters worse Daniel takes over the practice. Then she learns Melissa Harper is back on the scene . . .

NOT AS A COWARD

Lillie Howard

Adele Price, after a sheltered Victorian upbringing with her kindly aunt and uncle in Wiltshire, longs for a challenge in life. Then she meets Philip Belvedere, and after a whirlwind courtship, they marry. Philip takes her back to Sadura, his home town in south-west India, and Adele is indeed challenged. The house is dominated by Philip's old ayah, and Philip's behaviour seems strange and deceitful. Meanwhile, it's David Baxter, the local doctor, who helps Adele to face her troubles . . .